THE FRIENDSHIP PROMISE

a novel

Umm Zakiyyah

AL-WALAA
PUBLICATIONS

THE FRIENDSHIP PROMISE
A Novel
By Umm Zakiyyah

Original copyright under *A Friendship Promise* by Ruby Moore.

ISBN: 978-1-942985-01-3

Library of Congress Control Number: 2016932610

Order information available online at
uzauthor.com and **ummzakiyyah.com/store**

Verses from Qur'an taken from Saheeh International, Darussalam,
and Yusuf Ali translations.

Published by Al-Walaa Publications
Camp Springs, Maryland USA

Front cover photography: Shutterstock © by dboystudio
Back cover photography: Shutterstock © by Andresr

ACKNOWLEDGEMENTS

It is certainly a tremendous blessing to have so much support and inspiration before a work is complete. For this story, I am grateful to my former students who listened eagerly to my read-aloud story "Who Am I?" that inspired this book. I am also grateful to my husband for the inspiration and encouragement to write for young adults, and to our daughter Fareedah, who read, edited, and critiqued this book every step of the way. And as always, I'm indebted to my parents whose lessons about life and the soul are in every stroke of my pen. May Allah reward and bless you all.

For the Muslim youth, whose scrutinizing judgment and endless questions force us to search deep within ourselves and offer better answers.

~

"I asked the Prophet, peace be upon him, 'Which deed is the most beloved to Allah?' He replied, 'To offer the prayers at their proper times.' I asked, 'Then what?' He replied, 'To be good and dutiful to your parents.'"
—Abdullah ibn Mas'ud (Bukhari)

~

"In this world, there is a paradise. Whoever does not enter it will not enter the Paradise of the Hereafter."
—Ibn Taymiyyah

PROLOGUE

Maryam's Thoughts

Have you ever asked yourself "Who am I?" or "What am I doing with my life?"

Yeah, I know they're boring questions, the kind your parents always want you to "ponder." And they're typical, I know. Too typical. And hey, I'll be honest, I didn't think about them much a few years ago.

And honestly, I still don't.

Okay, but seriously, I think about this stuff more than I used to. Sometimes when I get all sad with how my life is, I say to myself, "Girl, do you even know who you are?" But when the question really gets to me, you know, when I can't figure out the "right" answer, I just shrug it off. I mean, I feel stupid talking to myself like that, even if it's just in my head.

But I can't help it. The question really bothers me.

And I think it's all because of Samira.

But if she'd ever catch me worrying over these silly "questions of life," she'd say, "Dummy, why are you stressing so much? The night is young, and we are young, so let's have some fun!"

Even now, I can't help laughing to myself when I think of her.

If anybody else had called me "Dummy," I wouldn't have liked it one bit. But with her…It was different.

Well, honestly, when she first said it, I was annoyed. But I eventually came to love it.

Just like I eventually came to love Samira.

You see, Samira's my best friend. …Well, she used to be.

Oh, Samira, how I hope to get back in touch. I miss you soooooo much!

1

A New Friend

"Sooo," the girl with hazel eyes said, "is your mom forcing you to hang out with me too?"

The girl yanked off her small white one-piece *khimaar* and tossed the head cover onto Maryam's desk. She mussed her dark hair that was trimmed to her earlobes, where gold-loop earrings dangled, and plopped onto the edge of Maryam's bed. The girl wrinkled her nose, making Maryam self-conscious of her own plain dark eyes and limp hair that she always wore in a single braid though Maryam had no idea what was disgusting the girl.

"Dummy!" The girl stared at Maryam with exaggerated widened eyes. "I'm talking to you."

Maryam drew in a deep breath from where she stood next to her closet, arms folded across her chest. She exhaled as she got up the nerve to take a few steps toward the bed. Her lips spread into a strained smile as she extended her hand to the girl.

"I'm Maryam."

The girl surprised Maryam by smiling in kind—unrestrained.

"I'm Samira." The girl shook Maryam's hand so effusively that Maryam's body jerked with the motion. The girl withdrew her hand to glance around at the walls of the bedroom.

"How can you live like this?" Samira said, wrinkling her nose again. "If I don't see Justin Bieber looking back at me, I get depressed."

Maryam turned and walked over to her desk, where she picked up the white cloth that Samira had deposited there, and she folded it carefully before laying the hijab neatly on the dresser.

"We don't hang pictures." Maryam slid into her desk chair and forced a smile that she knew would allow Samira to catch the sarcasm in her words.

Samira rolled her eyes. "Oh my God. Fundamentalists. I should've known my mom wouldn't let me hang around normal Muslims."

Maryam's cheeks colored. But she wasn't going to let this girl get the better of her. "*Normal* Muslims don't hang pictures."

"Oh I'm sorry." Samira raised her hands as if surrender. "I meant I should've known my mom wouldn't let me hang around *abnormal* Muslims like me."

Maryam sighed aloud, realizing Islam wasn't a safe subject if they were going to get along. "Do you have any hobbies or anything?" Maryam said. "Like drawing or painting or cooking?"

Samira brought her eyebrows together as a smirk formed on her face. "So it's okay to *draw* pictures, but it's not okay to—"

"*As-salaamu'alaikum,*" a voice called out in a song-like tone as the room door opened.

Maryam's face brightened and she nearly leaped from the chair and embraced her friend with a warm hug.

"Wooooe," Latifah said, laughing as she pulled away from Maryam. "What was that for?"

Maryam's face grew hot in embarrassment, ashamed that her relief at seeing a familiar face was so obvious. "I'm just happy to see you."

Latifah wrinkled her forehead, smirking. "Well, I'm happy to see you too." She chuckled. "But we just saw each other yesterday, remember?"

Maryam laughed self-consciously. "Yeah, I guess you're right."

"You must be Samira." Latifah walked over to where Samira was sitting and reached out a hand. "I'm Latifah."

"Cool," Samira said, shaking Latifah's hand as she stared at Latifah in awe. "Like Queen Latifah?"

Latifah grinned as she lifted her head slightly to unfasten the safety pin under her chin. The maroon cloth around her head immediately loosened until the smooth brown of her throat was exposed. She pulled the *khimaar* from her head and folded it, revealing rows of thin braids flat against her scalp and fading into a mass of small plaits at the back.

"Yeah," Latifah said, a smile playing at the corners of her mouth, "like Queen Latifah."

Latifah placed her folded hijab on top of Samira's and sat down on the bed next to Samira, still smiling in amusement as she looked at the new acquaintance.

"So you're from Saudi Arabia?" Latifah asked.

Samira wrinkled her nose. "No way. Who told you that?"

Latifah shrugged. "My mom."

Maryam slid back into her desk chair, her discomfort loosening a bit. "My mom told me the same thing," she said, her voice awkward in an attempt to be polite.

Maryam's mother had said that an old friend of hers who lived in Saudi Arabia was recently divorced and had moved back to the Washington, D.C.-Maryland area a month ago with her daughter.

Samira averted her gaze momentarily, and Maryam sensed Samira was uncomfortable with the topic. "I don't know where they got that from," Samira said. "We lived there, but I'm not *from* there."

"Well, I'm from Pakistan," Maryam said, smiling.

"And I'm from New York," Latifah said.

"I'm Desi too," Samira said, appearing to relax somewhat. She smiled.

Latifah looked confused momentarily, but she maintained her pleasant expression as she shook her head.

"Well, *I'm* not Desi. My parents are just regular Americans, but Maryam's—"

"Are you kidding?" Samira rolled her eyes and laughed heartily. "It's obvious you're not Desi. I was talking to Maryam."

Latifah laughed at the mix-up. "Good. I was about to say…"

Maryam smiled, a bit uncomfortable with the attention. "So have you ever lived there?"

"Where?" Samira asked.

"In Pakistan."

"No, have you?"

"No."

"So you lived in America all your life?" Samira's eyes glistened in admiration.

"Yeah. My parents moved to America before I was born."

"Cool."

"Well," Latifah said, chuckling, "I think it's cool that *you* lived in Saudi Arabia."

Samira shrugged, an uncomfortable expression on her face. "Saudi was okay. But I was born in Rockville, Maryland."

"How long were you in Saudi Arabia?" Latifah asked.

"Since I was seven."

"How old are you now?" Maryam looked at Samira, intense interest in her eyes.

"Fourteen. You?"

Maryam smiled. "Same."

"Are you fourteen too?" Samira's eyes widened slightly as she turned to Latifah.

"Almost," Latifah said, smiling. "I turn fourteen in September."

"Cool," Samira said. "We're all the same age."

"Yeah, that is cool," Latifah said. But Maryam sensed her friend was just trying to be polite.

"Who's your favorite singer?" Samira's eyes twinkled eagerly as she looked at Latifah.

Latifah appeared taken aback by the question, but she chuckled. "Zain Bhikha."

Samira furrowed her brows as her smile faded slightly. "Who?"

"Zain Bhikha." Latifah spoke if he was the most famous singer in the world. "You never heard of him?"

"No…" Samira looked slightly embarrassed. "Is he new?"

Latifah shook her head. "No, I don't think so. He's been around a while."

Samira was quiet, as if unsure how to respond.

"Who's *your* favorite singer?" Latifah asked, looking at Samira.

Maryam cringed, remembering Samira's Justin Bieber remark before Latifah arrived. She dreaded what Samira would say.

"Alicia Keys," Samira said.

The room grew quiet momentarily as Latifah studied Samira, a curious smile lingering on her face.

"I thought you liked Justin Bieber," Maryam said.

Samira shrugged. "I do. But he's not my favorite."

Latifah turned to Maryam, her expression a storm of question marks.

Maryam waved her hand dismissively and chuckled as she met Latifah's gaze. "We were discussing him when you came in."

"Oh…"

"Not like that!" Maryam laughed.

Latifah sighed and shook her head, amused. "I was about to say…"

"Don't tell me *you're* a fundamentalist too." Samira groaned, rolling her eyes.

Latifah blinked repeatedly. She wore a puzzled expression as she looked at Samira. She forced laughter. "What?"

"Maryam said that Muslims can't have pictures."

Latifah drew her eyebrows together as she looked at Maryam. "You did?"

"I said they don't *hang* pictures."

"Same thing," Samira said.

"It's not the same thing." Maryam felt herself growing annoyed.

"Whatever," Latifah said, waving her hand. "It doesn't matter."

An awkward silence followed as no one knew what to say.

"You want to hear my favorite Zain Bhikha album?" Latifah asked, grinning at Samira.

Samira's expression softened and she smiled. "Yeah, sure."

***

"All I'm saying, Basma, is I don't like the idea of our daughter playing babysitter for your friends."

It was almost midnight and Faris stood in the doorway to the kitchen with his arms crossed over his chest. The guests had gone home an hour before and his wife stood next to the trash can scraping chicken bones and remnants of rice from glass plates.

"Maryam's not playing babysitter, Faris. We're helping a Muslim sister do what we're all trying to do. That's all."

"Raise her daughter for her?" Faris huffed. "Parents usually raise their children, Basma. They don't ask little girls to help them out."

"Remember when Maryam was ten, and you asked me to enroll her in the weekend school so she could have Muslim friends?"

Faris sighed, his impatience thinly veiled in that sound. "That's not the same thing."

"It is the same thing." Basma walked over to the sink and set the plate on top of the others, her hair a thick braid securely at her back. "Joanne wants for her daughter what we want for ours."

Faris was silent as he ran his fingers through his beard.

"I believe that," he said. "I'm just not so sure an American divorcee has any idea what this will mean for *us*."

Basma's jaw stiffened, a shadow darkening her pale olive skin. "Don't be a bigot, for God's sake. Most American converts are better Muslims than people like us."

Faris groaned and shook his head. "You know what I believe about that. It's hogwash. They have no idea what Islam really is. You see most of them going from group to group, masjid to masjid, searching for so-called 'true Islam.' They dress like Arabs, think it's the Sunnah and—"

"Faris, please. Stop it." Basma unbuttoned the cuffs of her blouse then rolled up her sleeves before dipping her hands into the dishwater to begin cleaning the plates. "Anyway, the girl's father is from Pakistan."

"As you said a million times."

"Yes, because I knew that was the only way you'd let her in our home."

"The Bilals were just here tonight, in case you forgot."

Basma drew in a deep breath and exhaled. "Let's not go there," she said. "Because I remember quite distinctly what you thought of them when they were just 'Black Muslims' to you."

"So I guess since I'm not comfortable with Joanne, I'm racist against White Muslims now?"

"Faris," Basma said quietly, glancing at her husband over her shoulder as she lifted a plate from the dish water, "I didn't use that word, and neither should you."

"But that's what it boils down to, me being racist. Or a bigot, as you like to say."

"I say *don't* be a bigot, Faris. I didn't say you are one."

"Well, if being leery of having Americans in my house makes me a bigot, then that's a good thing."

"Faris, we're *Muslim*."

"And? Does being Muslim mean we shut our eyes and accept this 'everything goes' culture like most American Muslims do?"

"Look who's talking. Some of our own family don't even pray or cover. And they have mixed parties, with wine and music and everything else."

"That's because they're Americanized."

Basma turned away from the sink, her eyes widened. "Tell me you're joking, Faris. That didn't come from America. They do things like that in Pakistan too."

"Yes, I know. Because they love America."

Basma grunted and rolled her eyes. She turned back to the sink, shaking her head as she resumed washing dishes.

They were silent for some time.

"Look, Basma. I'm sorry." Faris sighed. "I know you're trying to do the right thing. I just don't want this girl corrupting our daughter. Joanne's family is not

Muslim." A concerned expression contorted his face. "And I don't want Maryam around anyone like that. It would be different if Joanne's family lived a different city, but they're practically down the street."

Basma was quiet for several seconds. "Maryam was in public school up until last year, Faris. I think it's a little late to worry about things like that."

"But she's not friends with non-Muslims, Basma. She's still innocent."

Basma drew in a deep breath and sighed. "Well, if you want me to tell Joanne that Samira can't come over anymore, I will."

Faris didn't respond immediately.

"But I don't agree with it," Basma said. "I highly doubt Samira's going to bring her Christian cousins over when she visits."

"It's okay," Faris said after some time. His voice was quieter, more thoughtful. "We can help them out. I'm sorry. I just don't want anything to happen to our daughter."

Basma turned to her husband, but his hands were deep in the pockets of his pants, his gaze on something beyond her. "Don't worry about that, Faris. She'll be fine, *inshaaAllah*. I'm sure about that."

Faris looked at his wife then. "What makes you so sure?"

She smiled. "Because I pray for Maryam every day. And Allah answers the prayer of the parent."

2

Friendship Style

"What do you think of her?" Maryam asked the following afternoon. She sat on her bed with her back supported by a pillow as she held the cordless receiver against her ear, her other hand studying the ends of some hair that had loosened itself from the braid.

"She seems nice, *maashaAllah*," Maryam heard Latifah say through the phone. "A bit different, but in a good way."

"Really?" Maryam raised her eyebrows as a smirk formed on her face. "I'm surprised you think so."

"Why? Because she likes Justin Bieber?" Latifah laughed. "That's not a big deal, if you ask me."

"I think it is."

"Because you're your father's child," Latifah teased.

Maryam frowned. She hated when Latifah said things like that. "Well, my father's right in how he feels."

"I didn't say he wasn't. I'm just saying you take after him."

"And you think that's a bad thing?"

Latifah's laughter crackled through the phone. "Oh come on. You're way too sensitive."

"And you're way too lenient."

"All I'm saying," Latifah said, laughter still in her voice, "it's not a big deal what singers she likes."

"Staring at Justin Bieber posters before going to sleep each night?" Maryam contorted her face at the phone. "That's creepy."

"And you think *you're* not creepy?" Amusement was in Latifah's tone.

Maryam grunted and rolled her eyes. "Why? Because I'm a 'normal Muslim'?"

"No, because you're an abnormal teenager."

Maryam was unsure what her friend meant, but her face grew hot in offense. She refused to respond, instead expressing her feelings by huffing into the phone.

"Don't act so surprised. You were called rag head in sixth grade, remember?"

At the reminder, Maryam's throat closed. She bit her lower lip. She didn't want to think about the year she started wearing hijab to school.

"Well, I don't see how that makes me abnormal," Maryam said.

"It makes us all abnormal, Maryam. I was called rag head too. My mom says that's just the way the world is. Muslims are weirdos now."

Maryam drew in a deep breath and exhaled. "It's not fair though."

"Life's not fair," Latifah said in a song-like tone.

"How can you joke about this? Doesn't it bother you how people treat us?"

Maryam heard Latifah sigh through the phone. "Oh, Maryam. Of course it bothers me. But my mom says sometimes laughter is the best medicine."

"Well, I wish I could see it how your family does. I don't see anything funny about being called a terrorist because I cover my hair."

"I didn't say it was funny, Maryam. I said sometimes laughing helps."

An awkward silence followed as each girl was lost in thought.

"You really should try laughing a bit more, girl," Latifah said, breaking the silence. "Life's really not all that bad."

Maryam sucked her teeth. "For you, maybe."

"For me?" The sound of Latifah's laughter made Maryam's cheeks grow warm in shame. "And how is my life better than yours?"

Maryam thought of Brother Hamid bursting into laughter after telling one of his own jokes. Meanwhile, Maryam's father would wear only a slight smile, restrained amusement on his face.

"It's not proper to laugh loudly like the Americans do," her father would often say. *"But what about just laughing?"* Maryam wanted to ask. *"Is that improper too?"*

"Your parents let you watch movies," Maryam said finally. She didn't want to share her true thoughts. She didn't understand them herself.

"Oh, puh-leez." Maryam could almost see Latifah rolling her eyes with those words. "You think we have movie night or something? My parents are way too strict about movies if you ask me."

"Watching *Incredibles* and *Kung Fu Panda* is better than nothing."

"I don't consider those movies, Maryam. They're toys come-to-life." Humor was in Latifah's voice.

"Do you really think I'm creepy?" Maryam asked. She drew her knees close to her as her eyes fell on the framed Qur'an poster of *Ayatul-Kursi* hanging above the flat screen monitor and printer on her desk.

"Of course not. What makes you ask something stupid like that?"

"I was thinking about Samira…"

"Oh, Maryam. Stop worrying yourself to death. The girl likes you. It's obvious."

Maryam rolled her eyes, a shy grin forming on her face. "Yeah right."

"I'm serious. She was so happy to say she's Desi like you."

"And…?"

"And if she's going Desi on you, then that's like total commitment."

Maryam burst into giggles despite herself. "Latifah, you're imagining things."

The sound of Latifah's laugh came through the receiver. "Well, I know how it is with Desi bonds. The glue works best when I'm not around."

"You don't mean that."

"Of course I do. I may be open-minded, Maryam. But I'm not stupid. I know a 'Keep Out' sign when I see one."

Maryam creased her forehead. "You really think Samira doesn't want you around?"

"Samira? Girl, Samira wouldn't care if I was purple." Latifah chuckled. "I'm talking about the Desi club in general. There are golden rules, you know."

Maryam smiled, shaking her head knowingly. "And what are those?"

"Rule number one," Latifah said, and Maryam could almost see her friend's eyes sparkling with humor right then. "Keep away from all non-Desis until they pass the 'Are they worth my time?' test."

Maryam rolled her eyes, still smiling. "And rule number two?"

"Oh that's easy," Latifah said. "If they're Black, no test needed. Stay away. For your own good."

"Ooooh," Maryam squealed in laughter. "You are so cruel."

Latifah was unable to keep from laughing herself.

"Who told you that?" Maryam said after recovering from laughter, a grin still on her face.

"The Arabic teacher at the weekend school."

Maryam brought a hand to her mouth. "Are you serious? I can't believe she'd say something like that."

"She didn't," Latifah said. "She was just so rude that I went home crying to my mother. That's when my mother translated everything for me."

Maryam was quiet momentarily, her expression growing serious. "Wow, I feel so bad for you."

"I don't," Latifah said, matter-of-fact. "Like my mom says, people like that are the ones you should feel bad for. Because if there's any crime in having dark skin, then they're picking a fight with Allah, not me."

***

"Please don't tell my heart, my achy breaky heart," Samira cooed, bobbing her head. A bright yellow iPod was in her right hand, a silver ring glistening from her ring finger. Her other hand was pressed against the side of her color-print *khimaar*, where an ear was hidden beneath the soft fabric, a thin white wire snaking from where the cloth framed her face.

"Samira," Maryam said with clinched teeth. She leaned close to Samira as she yanked Samira toward her by the elbow. "People are looking."

"…I just don't think he'd understand." Samira moved her shoulders rhythmically even as she was thrown off balance by Maryam's pulling. "And if you tell my—"

"Samira!"

Samira started, pulling the white wire from beneath her head cover until one iPod ear piece dangled awkwardly in front of her chest, the other still hidden and secure in her other ear.

Her eyes were wide when she looked at Maryam, who still held her by the elbow. "What happened?"

Maryam glared at her in response.

Samira blinked, her eyes still wide. "What?"

Maryam widened her own eyes. "You were singing, Samira," she said in a low voice. "Loudly."

Samira immediately looked around her from where they were walking in the mall.

"Did anyone hear me?" Samira whispered, quickly pulling the other ear piece from under the cloth then shutting off the iPod.

"Are you kidding?" Maryam said. "They probably think this is some cover-up terrorist operation."

"Singing in the mall?" Samira looked genuinely shocked. She wrapped the white cord around the iPod. "It's not allowed here or something?"

"Oh my God. Is that all you're worried about?" Maryam's hand went to her own dark grey *khimaar*, and she tugged self-consciously on her black *jilbaab*. "People were *staring* at us."

Samira appeared embarrassed as she glanced about again. Her gaze followed a young couple immersed in their own conversation. "I don't see anyone staring."

"Well, I *felt* them staring."

Samira wrinkled her nose knowingly. "Perverts, huh?"

"No… Normal people." Maryam let go of Samira's arm, shaking her head as she walked toward the pretzel kiosk.

"So what?"

"*So what?*" Maryam repeated in disbelief. "You don't mind making a complete fool of yourself?"

"What's so foolish about enjoying a song?"

"Nothing," Maryam said, "if it's to yourself."

Samira shrugged nonchalantly.

"At home," Maryam added, rolling her eyes.

"Gosh," Maryam said. "I would never have come here if I knew you'd make us look like complete idiots."

"Dummy, you're the only idiot here."

Maryam halted her steps before she reached the growing line in front of the soft pretzel shop. "Don't call me that."

"Well you are. Getting all worried about what people think of you." Samira's nose flared as she shook her head. "You're the last person I'd expect to worry about what people think."

Taken aback, Maryam creased her forehead. "What's that supposed to mean?"

"My mom talks about your family like you're from *Ahl-ul-Bayt* or something. So I thought you'd have more guts than that."

"*Ahl-ul-Bayt*?"

"The family of the Prophet."

Maryam rolled her eyes as her cheeks grew warm in embarrassment. "What does making yourself look stupid have to do with guts?"

"You're the only one looking stupid, Dummy."

Maryam started to say something, but Samira spoke before she could.

"If you're such a good Muslim, why do you care what people think?"

Maryam's mouth fell open, her face burning in humiliation. A thousand thoughts crossed her mind, but she couldn't settle on a single thing to say in defense of herself.

"Mmmm," Samira said, her eyes darting to a girl passing them right then.

Confused, Maryam followed Samira's gaze.

"That looks soooo good," Samira said.

That's when Maryam noticed the warm pretzel the girl was dipping in chocolate sauce.

"Let's get in line before it gets too long," Samira said, pulling Maryam by the arm.

"Wh…" Maryam said as Samira practically dragged her to the line.

"I think I'm getting caramel sauce with mine." Samira's eyes twinkled as she eagerly skimmed the choices mounted on the wall behind the workers. Samira turned to Maryam, releasing her arm. "What about you?"

To Maryam's surprise, Samira seemed sincerely interested in her response.

"Me?" Maryam was still recovering from offense at Samira's insult.

"Yes you, Dummy." Samira laughed and shook her head. She pulled the strap of her purse from over her shoulder and unzipped it before dropping the iPod inside.

"Did you bring money?" Samira asked, her expression more serious. "Because I can pay if—"

"I have money," Maryam said, rolling her eyes as she pulled her purse in front of her, the strap still on her shoulder.

"Good," Samira said, grinning, "because I want to buy extra for later."

***

Early that Saturday afternoon, Joanne sat on the couch in Basma's living room cradling a cup of tea with both hands. Her eyes were distant as she leaned forward and took a sip. She peered into the cup absently for several seconds.

"Thank you for what you're doing for Samira," Joanne said. The rich brown cloth of her *khimaar* framed her pale face and accented the hazel eyes she and her daughter shared. "It really means a lot to me."

Basma took a sip of her own tea from where she sat on the couch a comfortable distance from her friend. "It's what I would want someone to do for me."

A hesitant smile played at one side of Joanne's mouth before she looked at Basma. "You haven't changed, have you? I remember how idealistic you were in college, wanting everyone to work together and love each other."

Smiling, Joanne shook her head before her eyes grew distant again. "I envied you for that."

Basma's dark eyebrows rose as she grinned. "What in the world do I have worth envying?"

"Your heart," Joanne said softly. "That beautiful heart."

"*MaashaAllah*," Basma said.

"*MaashaAllah*," Joanne repeated, her voice just above a whisper.

"But you underestimate yourself, Joanne. You're about as kind as they come."

Joanne suppressed a cough of laughter as she swallowed a sip of tea. She reached forward and set her teacup on the glass of the floor table in front of them.

"Oh, Basma, if you only knew me now."

Basma was silent, a frown toying at the side of her mouth. She gazed at Joanne, a look of sympathy in her eyes.

"How are you, Joanne? Do you need anything? I mean, with the divorce and all…"

Joanne was quiet momentarily then lifted a shoulder in a shrug. "Prayers I suppose. Lots of prayers."

"But you're…okay?"

Joanne heard her friend's voice as if from a distance, and it tickled a small space on the left side of her chest. She drew in a deep breath to soothe the familiar burning sensation in her eyes. But she chuckled, betraying her true feelings. "I could use a shrink."

"Oh, Joanne," Basma said, stretching out her friend's name sympathetically. She set down her teacup and leaned to the side, placing a hand on Joanne's leg. "Don't talk like that. You're not crazy."

"So they say…"

Basma forced laughter. "Now you *are* talking crazy."

Joanne shook her head, her eyes glistening. "Basma, I keep asking myself over and over what I did wrong. I tried everything. I cooked. I cleaned. I even gave up my career…"

"Joanne, please don't do this to yourself."

"But I wasn't good enough." Tears welled in Joanne's eyes. "He said it wasn't me. It was just too much for his family to accept me." Her last words came out as a croak.

"Joanne—"

"But what does that mean, Basma? Tell me. I didn't care about where Riaz was from. I didn't care that we came from different worlds. I loved Riaz because he was Riaz."

"Joanne—"

"Why couldn't he love me because I was Joanne?" She heard the whine in her voice but couldn't contain herself.

"Oh, Joanne."

A second later Joanne felt warm arms embracing her, and she sobbed into the shoulder beneath the cotton *shawar khameez* that smelled of spices and laundry soap.

***

Later that evening Maryam sat opposite Samira on the carpeted floor of her bedroom after her mother had picked them up from the mall. Maryam stared curiously at Samira, who kept shutting her eyes as she lifted a purple can of soda to her mouth each time she took a sip.

"What was that song you were singing at the mall today?"

Maryam heard Samira gulp before responding.

"You mean 'Achy Breaky Heart'?" Samira's eyes remained shut until she finished the question. But her mouth still hovered over the can as she spoke.

"Yeah, I guess so."

"It's an old song my mom listens to."

Maryam's eyes widened. "Your mom listens to *music*?"

Samira lowered the can slightly as she furrowed her brows. "Yours doesn't?"

Maryam shook her head. "Never. It's *haraam*."

Samira blinked and looked as if she wanted to say something but shrugged her shoulders instead. Then she shut her eyes and lifted the can to her mouth again. She gulped loudly before giggling and looking at Maryam.

"What are you staring at?"

Self-conscious all of a sudden, Maryam turned away. "Nothing. I just…"

"Never saw anyone drink grape pop before?"

"Grape what?"

"Pop. Soda pop."

"You mean grape soda?"

Samira lifted a shoulder in a shrug. "Same thing."

"Oh…"

An awkward silence followed as Maryam didn't know what else to say.

"Billy Ray Cyrus," Samira said a few seconds later, shaking the can to see if any soda was left. She peered inside the can by shutting one eye then shut both as she lifted the can until it was upside down. She bent her head back as she poured the final drops on her tongue.

Maryam wrinkled her forehead. "What?"

Samira lowered the can as she opened her eyes again, her upper lip purple stained. Samira licked her lips just before an amused grin spread on her face.

"Billy. Ray. Cy-rus." Samira leaned forward, speaking as if talking to a child. "The singer, Dummy."

Maryam grimaced. "I wish you'd stop calling me that."

Samira creased her forehead, appearing sincerely puzzled. "Calling you what?"

"Dummy."

Samira blinked as the realization came to her. "Oh *that*." She waved her hand dismissively. "Get over yourself. It's nothing personal."

"Well, I don't like it."

"And I don't like you."

It took a few seconds for Maryam to register what Samira had said. She narrowed her eyes into slits as her heart thumped in her chest. "How *dare* you."

A loud burp escaped Samira's throat, and Samira immediately brought a hand to her mouth in apology. "Excuse me," she said, unable to restrain a giggle.

Maryam huffed and folded her hands over her chest as she rolled her eyes to the ceiling. "You are so disgusting, I swear."

Samira burped again, prompting Maryam to stare at her with wide eyes, as if saying *Are you serious?*

"Excuse me," Samira said again, this time cackling in laughter.

"Whew!" Samira said, waving her hand in front of her mouth. "That one smelled like sour grapes."

Maryam jumped to her feet and pointed to the door. "Get out of my room, you pig."

For a moment, the only sound that could be heard was Samira's laughter, which she was unable to restrain. But she burst into a new fit every time she caught Maryam's glare.

"Out!"

"Why?" Samira managed to ask after successfully suppressing laughter, but a grin was still on her face.

"You called me Dummy and burped in my room."

"And you called me a pig and said I'm disgusting."

Maryam's hand was still pointing to the door as she opened her mouth to reply. But in that moment, she realized Samira was right. She had said those terrible things.

"I'd rather be a dummy than a disgusting pig," Samira said, smiling up at Maryam. Her tone conveyed amusement.

Unsure what to say in response, Maryam stood with her hand still pointing defiantly to the door.

"Well…" Samira said after a few seconds of silence between them. "Are you just going to stand there like a crippled Statue of Liberty, or are you going to sit down and hear my heart-to-heart?"

Blinking in embarrassment, Maryam slowly lowered her arm to her side.

"I still don't want you here anymore," Maryam said, defiance in her voice, though considerably less so than before.

"Why? Because I said I don't like you?"

"Well…" Maryam pouted. "…yes."

"Why does it matter to you? You don't like me either, so we're even."

"I never said that."

"You didn't have to."

Maryam huffed, rolling her eyes. "Oh, so you read minds now?"

"No." Samira folded her arms as her smile faded slightly. "But I do read hearts."

Maryam wrinkled her nose as she regarded Samira. "Liar."

"Wanna bet?"

"I don't bet," Maryam said indignantly.

Samira rolled her eyes as her head followed the motion. "Well, excuse me for being such a *haraami*."

Maryam felt herself becoming more irritated. "A what?"

"*Haraami*. A bad girl. You know, someone who commits all these terrible sins. Lying, drinking, burping, betting…"

"I never said you drink."

"I meant grape soda."

Maryam grunted in frustration. "Don't make fun of your religion, Samira. It's *kufr*."

"What?" Samira's expression reflected genuine shock. "I'm making fun of *you*, Dummy. Not Islam." Samira folded her arms over her chest. "Or is that a sin in this house?"

"It's a sin in this room," Maryam said.

Samira groaned. "Oh for heaven's sake, Maryam, can you just shut up and sit down? I have something to tell you."

"Why should I, since you don't like me?"

"And why not, since *you* don't like *me*?"

Maryam's nose flared. "That's *not* true."

"Then prove it."

Maryam turned away from Samira and crossed her arms, struggling to gather her composure.

"If we're going to do Friendship Style," Samira said, "you have to uncross your arms and face me." Samira scooted closer to Maryam then folded her legs like a pretzel, one knee brazing Samira's ankle.

"Come on, Dummy," Samira said reaching for one of Maryam's hands, tugging it lightly. "It's like this."

Samira's fingers felt cool against Maryam's palm, and Maryam remembered the grape soda can Samira was holding earlier. Maryam felt stupid as a lump developed in her throat as she reluctantly obeyed Samira's urging.

"Now, here's how Friendship Style works..."

***

A single tear escaped Maryam's eyes and slowly rounded the side of her cheek until it was a moist spot on the soft pillow beneath her head. She lay on her right side, her body facing the wall in the darkness.

"Friends forever, friends forever, friends forever more."

Maryam could almost hear Samira's rhythmic whisper reciting the Friendship Style chant.

"Say it with me, Dummy," Samira had said with a giggle. Each of Samira's hands held one of Maryam's as Samira recited the chant.

"And close your eyes while you say it. Otherwise it's not a friendship promise."

"What am I promising?"

"Close your eyes and you'll see."

"But how..."

"Dummy, listen."

"To what?"

"This."

"Wh..."

"Friends forever, friends forever, friends forever more."

"Okay, but..."

"Just say it."

"O-kay..."

"On the count of three, okay? One, two, three..."

"Friends forever, friends forever, friends forever more." They had sat eyes closed, knees touching and hands grasped, as they recited the chant in unison.

"Now, it's sealed."

"What's sealed?" Maryam had asked, opening her eyes. But their hands remained loosely holding each other's.

"Our pact."

"What?"

"You see, Maryam," Samira had said, surprising Maryam by the use of her proper name. *"Anything we share in our heart-to-heart never leaves the room. Friendship Style is one heart talking to another."*

"But I thought we didn't like each other," Maryam said, a hesitant grin on her face.

"It doesn't matter," Samira said with a shrug. *"Our hearts can still speak to each other. And that's how we bond. Then we don't have to worry about liking each other."*

"Why not?"

"Because then we'll love each other, and it won't matter what you or I think."

3

Internet Standoff

"I can't believe you let Maryam have internet in her room." Joanne gripped the steering wheel with her left hand as she lifted a can of diet cola from the cup holder and took a sip. She shook her head as she held the can inches from her mouth. "I swear that's the one thing that makes me really uncomfortable when Samira comes over."

In her peripheral vision, Joanne could see Basma turn to look at her, but Joanne kept her eyes on the road. She already knew what her friend was thinking. It was what most Muslims thought when they heard her views on teens and internet usage.

"Really, Joanne," Basma said, shaking her head, "I'm surprised you feel that way."

"Why? Because I'm a bad Muslim and should just go all the way?" Joanne chuckled and shook her head before taking another sip of cola.

"I didn't say that."

"You didn't have to."

Joanne returned the can to its place and smiled at Basma.

"Don't worry," Joanne said. "I don't blame you for it. I'm used to people thinking I'm a hypocrite."

"Oh, Joanne, for God's sake. Can we talk about something else?"

"I didn't bring this up to bicker, Basma. I'm really worried about my daughter."

"And you don't think I'd treat her like my own?"

Joanne slowed the car to a stop behind a line of vehicles at a red light. "Honestly, Basma," she said quietly. "That's what I *don't* want you to do."

Joanne frowned apologetically as she met Basma's shocked gaze. "I'm sorry if it sounds like I'm being judgmental, but—"

"If anyone should be worried," Basma said, narrowing her eyes through the slits of her black face veil, "it should be me."

Joanne's eyes widened as she chuckled. "And what's that supposed to mean?"

"It means you're not the only one worried about her daughter."

"So you believe Samira will corrupt your innocent little girl?" Joanne rolled her eyes and smirked. "I should've known you'd see this whole thing as a one-sided charity case."

"Well, Faris and I *are* sacrificing a lot to help you."

Joanne drew her eyebrows together. "You and *Faris*? What does your husband have to do with anything?"

"Oh my God. You can't be serious, Joanne. Did you think I'd just invite some girl over to spend hours alone with our daughter and not ask his permission?"

"His *permission*?" Joanne looked at her friend, hands gripping the steering wheel. "You mean letting my daughter come over requires some major family deliberation?"

"Well, actually, it does."

Speechless, Joanne stared at Basma. It was only the sound of a beeping horn that prompted Joanne to blink and shake her head. She lifted her foot from the brake and rested it on the gas pedal, guiding the car past the green light.

"In an Islamic household," Basma said, her voice authoritative despite the soft tone. "that's how it should be."

"In an *Islamic* household?" Joanne contorted her face. "So what does that make *my* household?"

"Joanne, don't be unreasonable. I just want you to know it's not personal."

"But it is personal, Basma. It's very personal."

Joanne squinted her eyes as she glanced at her friend. "Think about it. Do you have to get permission every time Maryam's *cousins* want to drop by?"

"They're family, Joanne. That's different. We have to keep ti—"

"In *Islam*," Joanne said, her emphasis on the word intentionally sarcastic, "cousins aren't family. Otherwise, how did you and Faris get married?"

"Wh..." Basma's eyes widened, but Joanne could tell Basma didn't know what to say.

"And isn't it true," Joanne said, "your husband can forbid *family* from visiting if he thinks they'll cause harm?"

"Well...yes...but—"

"But nothing, Basma. So it's personal. Period. There's no need to lie about it." Joanne's nose flared. She shook her head. "And Islam forbids lying last time I checked."

Basma sighed, and Joanne sensed her friend wasn't in the mood to argue.

Joanne felt a tinge of guilt pinching her, but she found it difficult to let go of her offense. How could Basma think she was corrupt?

Joanne huffed. Was this what her life would forever be as a Muslim? Other Muslims holding her at arm's length? Admiring because she's American, but distrusting for the same reason?

Shaking her head, Joanne propped her left elbow on the seal of the window next to her as her right hand steered the car. Oh how she'd believed all that universal brotherhood rhetoric when she first accepted Islam. But now...what was left for her? Not even the marriage she'd thrown her heart into sustaining. She now lived an ocean apart from her youngest children—two boys she loved more than life itself.

Joanne was tired of hearing how Islam is perfect and Muslims are imperfect or how she shouldn't judge Islam by the actions of Muslims.

"Oh please," an American convert had said once, rolling her eyes. *"That's just what they say so they can keep living culture and ignoring Islam."*

At the time, Joanne had been infuriated. She was personally offended because she was married into one of the very cultures the woman was criticizing. "I swear to God these Black people are impossible," Joanne had said to Riaz later that day. "People bend over backwards to treat them equal, but it's never enough." Riaz had laughed in agreement as she continued venting. "They're a bunch of ungrateful leeches if you ask me. Always got their hands out, but then they complain that even the people who *help* them are racist!"

These were the words that hung in Joanne's mind as she pulled the car to a stop in front of the Muslim high school where the girls were finishing a placement exam.

Joanne felt the beginning of a headache. She was beginning to see the world with the very eyes she'd scorned for so long.

"Oh, sweetheart, don't blame yourself," Riaz had said when he'd sat her down to explain his reasons for divorce. *"It's not your fault. It's just that this has been really hard for my family."*

What the—? Joanne had thought at the time. Was he kidding? You're just going to throw away a marriage of fifteen years because your wife can't "fit in" the family? *You knew I couldn't speak Urdu or cook biryani when you married me!*

"Joanne," Basma's soft voice drifted to Joanne as if from a distance, "are you okay?"

Joanne's heart beat had slowed to a normal rate, but the tightening in her chest had not loosened.

It's not personal, Joanne.

Such simple, sincere words Basma had spoken. Yet they were eerily similar to the ones Riaz had used to break apart an entire family.

Yes, I know it's not personal, Basma, Joanne thought as she turned the keys to shut off the engine. *My problem is one I can't control.*

The keys jingled as she pulled them out the ignition.

I exist.

***

Faris lowered the newspaper he was reading and turned to glare at his wife from where he sat on the living room couch next to her. "And you actually promised this woman we won't have internet on while her daughter is here?"

Basma shrugged. "Yes…"

"And you think this is reasonable?"

"No, not really, but—"

"I swear, Basma. I have no idea why you put yourself through this." Faris moved his head toward her. "Mark my words, I think this little charity of yours is going to bring us more stress than it's worth."

"She's a good Muslim though…"

"Oh give me a break." Faris snapped the newspaper in place. "Listening to music? Going to movies? Walking around in front of men with her face exposed and wearing jeans and a hijab?" He shook his head as he resumed reading.

"But you don't mind?" Basma's tone was soft and tentative.

Faris groaned and lowered the paper again. "I mind, Basma, and you know that. In fact, I more than 'mind,' I completely disagree. The only reason I'm not forbidding this outright is I feel sorry for the woman."

"You mean letting my daughter come over requires some major family deliberation?"

Basma's cheeks grew warm in mortification.

Faris grumbled from behind the paper. "But I feel sorrier for the man who married her in the first place."

"Faris," Basma said, unable to keep from raising her voice. "You don't even *know* her."

"I don't need to know her, Basma. I see her. That's enough." He huffed. "I swear, I cringe at the thought of that gum-chewing, iPod-carrying girl coming anywhere *near* Maryam."

Basma sighed. She knew it was useless to suggest to Faris that he was backbiting Joanne's family. *"Not when she's doing these things openly,"* he'd say. *"The world sees what she's doing. I'm just saying I don't like it."*

"So what should we do about the internet?" Basma said. She didn't want to talk any more about the huge sacrifice they were making to help Joanne. It bothered Basma too much, and it was made all the worse because Joanne would blame her for even seeing it as a sacrifice.

Why are Americans so judgmental? It seemed to Basma as if they searched for prejudice.

"Thank you for what you're doing for Samira," Joanne had said. *"It really means a lot to me."*

But did it really?

Basma was already exhausted with the whole ordeal. What was she doing this for anyway? Her husband was right. This whole thing could end up harming Maryam…

"You figure it out," Faris said from behind the paper. "If you want my vote, I say we're stretching ourselves thin by even letting them in our house. Now they have the audacity to judge *our* lifestyle?"

***

Maryam was sitting at her desk in front of the flat screen monitor of her computer when she heard a light knock at her door. She glanced up to find the door that was slightly ajar opening wider.

"Are you busy?" Her mother said after stepping inside.

Maryam shook her head and nodded toward the monitor. "Just looking some things up for school."

Basma chuckled. "But school doesn't start for another two weeks."

Maryam smiled. "They said I should brush up on math."

"I don't think they meant during summer vacation."

"But I don't want to be behind when school starts."

"True enough."

Basma walked over to Maryam's bed and sat down, prompting Maryam to turn in her desk chair and face her mother.

"Ummi, is everything okay?" Basma looked a bit tired, and her eyes were slightly red.

Basma forced a smile. "I just wanted to ask how you and Samira are getting along."

Maryam averted her gaze as she thought of Friendship Style. She shrugged. "We're getting along okay."

Basma nodded, but Maryam sensed her mother had something else on her mind.

"Do you like her?"

Maryam started, her eyes widening slightly as she looked at her mother. *How did she know about the argument?*

A second later Maryam relaxed, realizing her mother was speaking in general.

"Um... I guess so."

"Does she like you?"

Maryam bit her lower lip, unsure how to respond. *And I don't like you.* The reminder of what Samira had said made a lump develop in Maryam's throat.

"Never mind." Basma waved her hand. "What's important is you're getting to know each other. That's how friendships begin. Allah is in charge of hearts."

Because then we'll love each other, and it won't matter what you or I think.

Maybe that's what Samira had meant. *Allah is in charge of hearts.*

"But we'll have to make some ground rules."

Maryam creased her forehead as she looked at her mother. "Ground rules?"

"For when Samira comes over."

Oh...

"Because her mother doesn't want her on the internet." Basma's lips formed a thin line as she attempted to smile, but Maryam sensed sarcasm in her mother's tone.

"But...why?"

"I suppose Sister Joanne thinks it's inappropriate for teenagers to be online."

Maryam contorted her face. She thought of Samira singing loudly at the mall, and a giggle crawled in her throat. Was Sister Joanne serious? The *internet* was inappropriate? But Maryam controlled her laughter. She didn't want her mother to scold her for being disrespectful.

Basma's smiling eyes and forced grimace conveyed she was fighting the same feeling as her daughter.

"Please don't tell my heart, my achy breaky heart."

Maryam had practically bullied Samira into not dancing through the halls of the mall bellowing a stupid *kaafir* song while iPod headphones dangled from the *khimaar* that barely covered Samira's chest.

And they needed ground rules for the internet? Oh my God.

Maryam's and Basma's eyes met, and Maryam cackled in an effort not to burst into giggles. Basma looked away, her own shoulders jerking in an effort to suppress an outburst.

Laughter was still in Basma's voice when she was finally able to control herself enough to speak.

"So we have to respect Sister Joanne's wishes, Maryam."

Maryam's lips formed a poorly restrained grin. "Yes, I know."

"Seriously." Basma narrowed her eyes in an effort to convey that she wasn't joking, but this only made Maryam break into giggles.

"Ummi," Maryam whined, humored.

"Okay, fine." Basma chuckled herself. "I admit that it makes absolutely no sense to me. And given Samira's—" Basma stopped herself.

A second later Basma sighed regretfully, an awkward smile on her face. "I'm sorry, Maryam, I just—"

"It's okay, Ummi. I understand." Maryam smiled at her mother, relieved she no longer had to hide her feelings.

Basma drew in a deep breath and exhaled.

"Look, it's late," Basma said, standing. "I'll let you finish your...homework."

Maryam turned her body toward the monitor as her mother walked to the door, the shadow of a smile still on Maryam's face.

"But make sure you're not on the internet when Samira is here."

Maryam's expression was a pout as she looked at her mother. "Never?"

"Let's put it like this," Basma said from the doorway, her eyes exhausted. She brought a hand to her head to smooth down her hair. "Officially, internet isn't allowed while she's here. But I can't say *never* get online if Samira is here." She shook her head, her hand now adjusting the chiffon *dupatta* covering her chest. "Because that's too much to ask. So if you need to get online, get online. But Samira isn't allowed to."

Maryam shrugged, turning to the screen, her hand on the mouse that she shook gently. "What if she asks to use the computer?"

Basma tucked a stray hair strand behind her ear. "Then the answer is no."

Maryam contorted her face, her gaze on the monitor that glowed back to life. "That sucks."

"*Maryam.*"

Maryam brought a hand to her mouth, her wide eyes in apology as she glanced at her mother. "Sorry. I mean, that's…too bad."

Basma shook her head, sadness in her expression. "I agree. But we have to respect Sister Joanne's rules."

"I didn't know she had any," Maryam mumbled to herself, tapping the keyboard as she keyed the words *pre-algebra practice* into the Google search engine.

"But I don't expect you to police Samira," Basma said, apparently having not heard her daughter's remark.

"And between you and me," Basma said with a grunt, "I couldn't care less if Samira surfs the net. That's the least of our worries."

"Okay." Maryam smirked in agreement, clicking the blue title of a math site on the screen. "I'll make sure she doesn't go online."

The awkward silence that followed prompted Maryam to look toward her mother. She found her mother's eyes glistening, a smile lingering on Basma's face.

"I love you, Maryam," Basma said. *"BarakAllaahufeek.* I'm really happy to have a daughter like you."

***

"I just can't afford it right now," Joanne said. She held the receiver between her shoulder and ear as she stirred a small pot of soup in front of the stove in her kitchen. She wore a faded pink night robe and fluffy slippers, her brown hair pulled back by a ponytail holder.

"Basma," Joanne said with a sigh after her friend protested, "I understand how important Muslim school is, but you heard what they said. There's no financial aid available."

"But what about Samira?" Basma's voice crackled through the phone.

Joanne groaned, the familiar fury building in her chest. "You know what, Basma. Let me worry about that. I'm her mother."

"I'm sorry, Joanne, but I'm just really concerned."

Joanne rolled her eyes. "About Samira or Maryam?"

"Both of them."

"Look," Joanne said, stirring the soup vigorously as she spoke. "I'll make this easy for you. Samira just won't come over your house anymore."

"Oh Joanne, that's not what I meant."

"Basma, I'm not stupid. I can read between the lines."

"But in this case, you're reading *into* the lines."

"Oh, please," Joanne said. "You've made it clear that you're making a huge sacrifice by even *befriending* me, so it doesn't take a rocket scientist to figure out why you're *really* worried about Samira going to public school."

"Okay, maybe I am a bit worried about how it will affect Maryam."

Joanne shook her head and raised her eyes to the ceiling, her gaze briefly resting on a small water stain. There was so much renovation her house needed. She had stayed away too long…

"But tell me, Basma," Joanne said, "exactly how will public school affect Maryam if she's not even there?"

Basma sighed through the phone. "You know what I mean."

"So now you're admitting this is really about protecting Maryam and not Samira?"

"What if it is? You think this is easy for me and Faris?"

What? Joanne turned off the stove and shifted the pot to another burner. Her heart pounded as she lifted the stirring spoon from the pot and tapped it against the side to release the remaining soup from it.

"Basma." Joanne clinched her teeth as she dropped the spoon into the sink. "Thank you for everything. But right now, I want you out of my life."

Hands trembling, Joanne pressed the off button as she grimaced at the cordless phone.

"You think this is easy for me and Faris?"

Joanne threw the phone against the wall, the crashing sound making her start. Tears welled in her eyes as she watched the gutted phone plop into the sink and slowly disappear into the dirty dishwater.

4

Something's Missing

"We are in high school now." Latifah hugged herself with her free arm as the wire of the phone twisted and stretched behind her in her bedroom. "Can you believe it?"

It was late Monday afternoon in early September, and school had been in session two weeks.

"I wish you were at the Muslim school," Maryam said through the receiver.

Latifah rolled her eyes. "Let's not go there. You know what my parents think about that."

"Maybe you can change their mind."

Latifah pulled the phone away from her ear, contorting her face and staring at the phone as if it were Maryam herself. One hand was on her hip as she put the phone back to her ear.

"Do I look like an idiot to you? Why pay four hundred dollars a month for insults, bullying, and discrimination when I can get that at public school for free? That's what my mom says."

"At least you'll be around Muslims."

"Can't argue with that," Latifah said with a shrug. "But it sure hurts more when it's Muslims, to tell you the truth."

Maryam was silent for so long that Latifah feared they had gotten disconnected.

"Hello?"

"I'm still here." Maryam's voice sounded sad and distant. "I'm just wondering what I'll do if my mom forbids me from talking to you."

Latifah wrinkled her nose. "Now what on earth are you talking about, girl?"

Maryam sighed. "I'm not allowed to talk to Samira anymore."

Latifah was silent momentarily. "You mean that Desi girl who used to live in Saudi?"

"Yeah."

"Why? What'd she do?"

"My mom says her mother put her in public school."

Latifah blinked repeatedly, a smirk forming on one side of her mouth. "And…?"

"And nothing. So Ummi thinks she'll corrupt me or something."

Latifah burst into laughter. "If that ain't the stupidest thing I ever heard."

"I'm serious. That's why she can't come over anymore."

"So…" Latifah squinted her eyes, a grin lingering on her face. "…you think your mom will say the same about me?"

"Yes."

Latifah sighed, her expression growing more concerned as she registered what her friend was saying. "Do you really think she'd do something like that? With me, I mean?"

"Why not? She did it with Samira."

Latifah felt her chest tighten in anxiety. She would hate to lose Maryam's friendship. They'd known each other since third grade.

"Maybe it's not because of public school," Latifah said thoughtfully. "I wasn't in Muslim school last year. If that was the reason, your mom would've said something by now."

The line went silent for several seconds, and Latifah sensed Maryam was thinking about what she'd said.

"I think it's because her mom's divorced," Latifah said. "And because they listen to music and stuff."

"Divorced?" Maryam chuckled. "What's that got to do with anything?"

Latifah lifted a shoulder in a shrug. "You tell me. My mom says immigrant Muslims get all superstitious about divorced women."

Maryam laughed. "And you say *we're* always stereotyping *you* guys?"

The sides of Latifah's mouth creased in a smile. "Yeah... That's true." She shrugged. "I guess we're all prejudiced, huh?"

"Guess so," Maryam said. But Latifah could tell she meant it in good humor.

"Should I ask her?" Maryam said.

Latifah drew her eyebrows together. "Ask who what?"

"My mom. About Samira."

"Why not?" Latifah shrugged. "I think you deserve to know." She paused. "But wait, I thought you said she said it's because of public school."

"But maybe I misunderstood."

"Yeah...maybe."

"So..." Maryam said, humor in her tone, "...there's no chance you'll be registering at the Islamic academy?"

Latifah laughed. "That'll be the day."

"You really don't want to go to school with Muslims?"

"Of course I do. I just don't want to be made fun of because I have brown skin."

"They don't do that in public school?"

Latifah detected genuine curiosity in Maryam's voice. She sensed Maryam needed to believe non-Muslims did worse.

"I can't say they don't," Latifah said. "But it never happened to me."

"Never?" Maryam's tone was of awed disbelief.

"Never."

"What about hijab?"

Latifah waved a hand in the air and rolled her eyes. "Let's not go there. Does 'rag head' ring a bell? Don't remind me."

Latifah heard Maryam breathe through the phone, and she couldn't tell whether it was because Maryam had bad memories of public school herself or because she was relieved that terrible things happened in public schools.

"Latifah?" Maryam's voice was tentative, as if unsure of something.

"Yeah?"

"If Muslims weren't so prejudiced, would you come back to Muslim school?"

Latifah drew in a deep breath and exhaled. The truth was, part of her wanted to come back anyway, even with all the racism and teasing. It wasn't easy walking around a public high school wearing a *khimaar* and *jilbaab*, which she was sure looked to the students like some ridiculously oversized dress.

Latifah hated herself for thinking it, but it bothered her that none of the boys would even notice her because of how she dressed. She felt so ugly and rejected next to all the girls with neatly styled hair and fitting clothes.

Latifah was beginning to wonder if Muslim school had been all that bad after all.

"Yes," she said with a sigh. "Honestly, I would."

***

"...So Crispus Attucks was the first to die for American independence..."

Tuesday morning, Latifah sat in U.S. history class with her head propped up by a fist against her cheek. She stifled a yawn as she doodled in the margins of her notebook.

"…What makes Attucks's legacy so dynamic is that he was actually a black slave."

Latifah halted her doodling and narrowed her eyes toward the front of the room. Had she heard the teacher correctly? Other students looked as surprised as Latifah was. They looked around at each other with quizzical expressions.

The teacher chuckled. "That's right. America's first martyr in the American Revolution was a black man."

Latifah studied the teacher's dark eyes and pale peach complexion that was framed by a closely trimmed beard. What was his background? He definitely wasn't Black…

"I never heard of him," a student said, his tone suggesting that he thought the teacher was making this all up.

"You have internet at home, young man?"

"Yes…"

"Google him, and see what you come up with."

The boy contorted his face but clamped his mouth shut. Latifah sensed the student feared having an extra homework assignment.

"This week," the teacher continued casually, "we're going to study the dynamics of the revolution and why it happened in the first place. What this means is—"

The classroom door opened, and the teacher stopped talking midsentence to look toward the door.

"Is this…U.S. History 101?" a girl asked tentatively, glancing uncertainly at a white slip of paper in her hand.

Latifah did a double take. The girl was wearing hijab.

"Yes it is," the teacher said, smiling broadly. He took the slip of paper from the girl and gestured toward the desks that were arranged in a semicircle. "Please take a seat."

The girl bit her lower lip and glanced around the room. The girl caught Latifah's gaze and did a double take herself.

Wait… Latifah thought. *I know those eyes.*

The girl smiled as she appeared to recognize Latifah at once.

Samira?

Latifah looked to her left and right, but both seats were taken.

"She can take my seat," the girl on Latifah's right said, standing and gathering her books.

Latifah knew why the girl gave up her seat, but Latifah wasn't offended. For once the stereotype was correct. The Muslim girls did want to sit next to each other.

"*As-salaamu 'alaikum*," Samira whispered, leaning toward Latifah as she slid into the seat. A broad grin was on her face.

"*Wa-'alaiku-mussalaam*," Latifah whispered back, grinning in return. "Why are you two weeks late to school?"

Samira rolled her eyes. "Saudi Arabia. They had my school records all messed up."

"So for the rest of the week," the teacher said, prompting Latifah and Samira to look forward, and Latifah was surprised to find the teacher smiling at her and Samira, "we'll be covering the American Revolution. You will read chapters one and…"

***

"Miss Bilal and Miss Saadiq," the history teacher called out over the commotion of students rushing out the class after the bell rang.

Latifah started. She halted arranging her notebook in her backpack as she lifted her gaze to the teacher.

She and Samira exchanged uncertain glances.

The teacher chuckled as he motioned with his hand for them to come to his desk. "It's okay. You're not in any trouble."

Some students who were making their way to the door glanced curiously at Latifah and Samira before leaving the room.

When the last students had shuffled out, the teacher sat on the edge of his desk and crossed his arms over his chest. Latifah and Samira stood in front of him, their expressions awkward.

"So you're Samira Riaz Saadiq?" he asked, his smiling eyes on Samira.

"Yes..." Samira said, stealing a glance at Latifah before turning her attention back to the teacher.

"Is your father Riaz Saadiq, the computer engineer who left to Saudi Arabia some years ago with his wife and children?"

Samira's jaw fell open in surprise.

The teacher laughed. "I'll take that as a yes."

"You have brothers and sisters?" Latifah asked, her forehead creased as she looked at Samira.

"No, just two brothers. They live with my dad."

A smirk formed on the side of Latifah's mouth. "That's cool. I do too."

"Really?" Samira looked genuinely surprised.

"Well," the teacher said, lifting the palms of his hands as he smiled, "don't let me intrude. I just wanted to see if it was luck or coincidence that I saw my old friend's name on my roster."

Samira regarded the teacher curiously. "You were friends...with my *dad*?"

"Briefly."

"Oh…"

"That's so *cool*," Latifah said, breaking into a grin.

"I'm Mr. Butt, by the way."

Samira and Latifah stared at the teacher uncertainly, their eyes growing wide.

Mr. Butt laughed. "Now you know why I didn't write it on the board."

"Are you…I mean…" Latifah said. "You're serious?" She had no idea how she'd sat in class for two weeks and didn't pick up on that name.

"I'm very serious." He maintained a pleasant expression. "I didn't have any problems with it in Pakistan, but here, it's quite a stir."

"You're from Pakistan?" Samira's eyes grew even wider.

Latifah rolled her eyes as laughter escaped her throat. "Oh no, here we go with the Desi club."

"It's quite a lot of us, huh?" Mr. Butt said.

"Too many if you ask me," Latifah said jokingly.

Mr. Butt laughed. "I can't say I disagree with you."

"Were you really friends with my father?"

Mr. Butt's eyebrows rose as he drew in a deep breath and exhaled. "We weren't close, but he left an impression."

Samira looked uncertain.

"In a good way," Mr. Butt said.

Samira smiled shyly.

"*MaashaAllah*," Latifah said, imagining how cool Samira's father must be.

"Yes, *maashaAllah*," Mr. Butt said with a nod.

"You're *Muslim*?" Latifah's eyebrows were drawn together as a disbelieving smile formed on her face.

Mr. Butt looked confused momentarily, but his expression remained. "Yes. Most Pakistanis are."

Latifah's smiled widened as she turned to Samira. "Wait till Maryam's mom hears about *that*."

"I'm sorry?" Mr. Butt said, his forehead creased.

"Maryam is Samira's friend," Latifah said, casually glancing at Mr. Butt then Samira. "But Maryam's mom won't let Maryam talk to Samira anymore because she thinks Samira will be a bad influence because she goes to public school." Latifah smirked. "Wait till she finds out we have a Muslim teacher—from Pakistan."

Samira's eyes grew large. "*What*?"

Latifah frowned as she looked at Samira. It took a moment for Latifah to understand the hurt in Samira's eyes. "Didn't Maryam tell you?"

"No..." Samira's tone was defiant, and Latifah immediately regretted what she had said.

"I'm sorry, I..."

Samira's nose flared as turned and stomped to her desk, where she retrieved her bag.

"Samira, wait." Latifah reached out a hand, trailing behind Samira. "I honestly thought you knew." Latifah watched helplessly as Samira yanked the zippers closed on her backpack.

"I *hate* Desis," Samira said as she pulled a strap of her bag over her shoulder.

Latifah took a step back at the words, her eyes narrowed in confusion. "Wh... Why?"

"They're a bunch of self-righteous punks!"

"Woe, woe, woe," a deep voice came from the front of the room.

Latifah turned to find Mr. Butt standing and waving his palms at them.

"Hold on a minute," he said. "I think it's a good idea if you take a second to pull yourself together before you go out there."

He walked to the classroom door and closed it before turning to face Latifah and Samira, his arms crossed authoritatively.

"I know you're upset, Miss Saadiq," he said. "But trust me." He gestured his head toward the door behind him. "That's not where you want to be if you need a good cry."

At his last words, Samira halted her steps, remembering just then where she was. Tears glistened in her eyes, and she quickly wiped them away with the back of her hand.

Latifah rushed to Samira's side and guided her to a desk as Samira's shoulders slouched, her backpack sliding to the floor in a thud.

"Here," Mr. Butt said as he walked quickly to his desk and opened a drawer. "I have some cola."

Samira's knees seem to give out as she sat down.

There was a popping and sizzling sound as Mr. Butt opened the can and handed it to Samira. Samira accepted the drink and slowly took a sip, but her eyes were dazed.

"Do you think she needs a nurse?" Latifah asked, turning to Mr. Butt, concerned.

"Hmm… Let's give her a few minutes. I may have to take her to the counselor though. Your words seemed to have triggered a difficult memory…"

***

Latifah's heart was heavy in regret as she leaned her head against the glass of the school bus window that afternoon. The engine hummed and grumbled as she grew lost in thought from where she sat a few seats behind the bus driver.

Why do you talk so much? Latifah scolded herself. She wished she hadn't opened her big mouth. If she'd kept her thoughts to herself, then maybe none of this would have happened.

Thank God Samira opened up to Mr. Butt. Latifah knew Samira would've never wanted to talk to a school counselor.

"I think I know how you feel," Mr. Butt had said after Samira divulged her parents' divorce and that it happened because her mother wasn't Pakistani. She also mentioned how her forced friendship with Maryam had been suddenly cut off.

Mr. Butt had pulled his desk chair in front of Samira, and Latifah sat next to her, unsure whether she should stay or leave. It was a blessing that it was lunchtime and no classes were in session. Otherwise, things wouldn't have worked out as they had.

"My parents nearly disowned me when I told them I wanted to be a teacher." He chuckled. "Of history of all things."

"Really?" Samira had asked, her eyes blinking in intense interest though her voice was weak.

"I was supposed to be a doctor."

"Why?"

"Because of my parents. My father's a doctor. My mother's a doctor. So I was supposed to be a doctor too."

"But why?"

"I suppose it's like you said. We Desis can be a bit self-righteous at times. Our culture doesn't believe in careers that don't bring honor to the family, especially for sons."

"So they just disowned you?" Samira found that difficult to believe.

"Not in the way Americans think of it. They still spoke to me. But I was a shame to the family."

"Why didn't you just become a doctor?"

Mr. Butt laughed. "I guess I'm supposed to have a really good answer to that. But to tell you the truth, I really don't know. I was young. I was hotheaded. History fascinated me, so I majored in it." He shrugged. "I didn't realize I couldn't do much with it until I couldn't find work."

"But what did you do?" Samira brought the can of cola to her lips, her eyes wide as she looked at Mr. Butt.

"I went back to school."

"Back to school?" Samira contorted her face. "Why?"

"Maybe I just needed to clear my head. I don't know. But I got my master's in African-American history."

It was Latifah's turn to be surprised. "You did?" It was the first question she'd asked.

"Yes, I did," he said, a distant look in his eyes that Latifah couldn't interpret.

"Wow...*maashaAllah*," Latifah said.

"But..." Latifah hesitated before speaking her thoughts aloud.

"Why?" he finished for her, smiling.

Latifah nodded, grinning.

"Black history fascinated me," he said honestly. "And with all I was going through with my parents...well, reading all those stories of people like Harriet Tubman and Fredrick Douglass and—"

"Crispus Attucks?" Latifah asked knowingly, her eyes sparkling.

He nodded, chuckling. "Yes. They made me realize I could persevere too."

"You could what?" Samira asked, her eyebrows drawn together.

"Persevere," he said. "Keep going, even though everything says you can't or shouldn't."

"Do you wish you were a doctor now?" Samira asked.

Mr. Butt's expression grew thoughtful. "Yes and no," he said finally. "Yes because I think it would make my parents proud, and no because I don't want to be a doctor." He forced a smile, but his eyes were sad. "Money and status aren't everything."

The bus whinnied as it came to a stop, and Latifah's body was jerked forward slightly. Latifah wondered what Samira was doing right then.

After the talk with Mr. Butt, Samira seemed more composed, and she attended the rest of her classes. But it bothered Latifah that the light was gone from Samira's eyes. Samira appeared drawn into herself in a way that didn't seem to fit her personality.

***

Saturday morning Basma woke to a loud pounding on the front door. She glanced at the clock and saw that it was 9:02. Groaning, she pulled the covers over her head.

But the pounding continued.

Who is *that?*

Basma sighed and sat up. She looked at her husband next to her, sound asleep. *If only I could sleep like that.* She rolled her eyes to the ceiling as she laid the back of her head against the headboard.

At the repeated ringing of the doorbell, Basma threw the covers from herself until her feet rested on the carpet of her bedroom floor. *What in the world?* Grumpy from irritation, Basma hurried downstairs, her cotton *shawar khameez* wrinkled from sleep.

"Who is it?" she called out near the door. Her hand went to her head as she realized she had forgotten her head cover.

At the door, she squinted through the peephole.

"It's me…Samira."

Basma's right hand immediately went to her heart.

What was *she* doing here?

Basma smoothed down stray hair strands with both hands then pulled at her *shawar khameez* to straighten it. She took a deep breath before unlocking the door and holding it open.

Samira stepped inside and stood in front of the door so that it remained ajar.

"*As-salaamu'alaikum*," Samira said. She frowned as she met Basma's gaze.

"*Wa'alaiku-mussalaam*." Basma's reply was hesitant, uncertainty written on her brow as she waited for an explanation for the unannounced visit.

For a few seconds, they just stared at each other, Samira's eyes red and withdrawn.

"Here." Samira averted her gaze as she held out a folded piece of paper.

Basma looked at the paper cautiously. "Is…this for Maryam?"

Samira grimaced. "No. I'm not allowed to talk to her, remember?"

Basma winced. The girl's expression was accusing, reminding Basma of a child threatening a tantrum.

"Did your mother send this?" Basma took the folded paper from Samira's hand.

"No. My mom's sleeping. She doesn't know I'm here."

"Then….?"

"I wrote it for you."

Basma blinked in shock. She glanced at the paper in her hand, unsure she should accept it. But before she could respond, Samira turned and walked out, pulling the door closed behind her.

Basma went to the window and peered through the curtains as Samira disappeared down the street, appearing troubled and lost in thought.

"I'm not allowed to talk to her, remember?"

The words came back to Basma suddenly, and her face flushed in offense.

How dare Joanne lie to her daughter. Basma's hand trembled as she let go of the curtain. *Joanne was the one who cut* me *off.*

Instinctively, Basma walked to where the phone sat on a small table next to the couch. Still holding the folded paper, she picked up the phone and dialed Joanne's number with shaking hands.

Heart pounding, she held the cordless receiver to her ear and paced the living room. The voicemail picked up after the fifth ring.

"Hi, this is Joanne," Joanne's too-perky recorded voice spoke through the receiver. "Sorry I missed your call..."

Annoyed, Basma disconnected then pressed redial.

When the voice mail picked up again, Basma started to hang up but stopped herself.

"...Please leave a message," Joanne's recording said.

At the beep, Basma drew in a deep breath, her heart pounding as she thought of Samira's accusing glare.

"Next time you want to play victim," she said, "try telling the *truth.*"

Basma hung up and walked over to the table and returned the receiver to its base. She had half a mind to drive the two blocks to Joanne and pound on her door, waking her as Samira had done.

Basma was halfway up the stairs when she glanced down, remembering the folded note in her hand.

Basma slowed her steps and unfolded the paper, her eyes eagerly grazing its contents.

I just wanted to say I forgive you because I know you can't help who you are. You think public school makes me a bad person so I feel sorry for you. Here's something I read that made me realize you don't understand Islam like you think you do: "Whosoever removes a worldly grief from a believer, Allah will remove from him one of the griefs of the Day of Judgment. Whosoever alleviates [the lot of] a needy person, Allah will alleviate [his lot] in this world and the next. Whosoever shields a Muslim, Allah will shield him in this world and the next. Allah will aid a slave [of His] so long as the slave aids his brother" (Muslim). I met a real Muslim at public school and he told me about this hadith. I hope you can become a real Muslim too.

5

A Truce

"Friends forever, friends forever, friends forever more." Eyes shut, Samira, Maryam, and Latifah chanted in unison and held each other's hands as they sat in a circle on the carpet of Maryam's bedroom floor. It was a Saturday evening in mid-November, two months from the day Samira had left the angry note with Maryam's mother.

Samira opened her eyes first, but she still held Maryam's and Latifah's hands.

"Now," Samira said, grinning as she raised her voice. "Time for heart-to-heart."

Maryam and Latifah giggled as their eyes fluttered open.

"Wait," Samira said, jumping to her feet and letting go of her friends' hands abruptly. She grabbed her backpack that lay near Maryam's desk chair. "Let's pray first."

Maryam and Latifah exchanged puzzled expressions.

"What time is it?" Samira said, looking at her friends as she unzipped her bag and pulled out a bundle of white floral cloth.

Maryam glanced at her wristwatch. "Five-oh-six."

"Then we're late for Maghrib," Samira said.

Maryam creased her forehead. "It just came in ten minutes ago."

"Then we're late." Samira shook the cloth then pulled the one-piece prayer garment over her head. Her voice was muffled momentarily as she pushed her arms through. "Come on. We can do Friendship Style after prayer."

Maryam rolled her eyes. "Relax. Prayer isn't about to go out any time soon."

Samira drew her eyebrows together and frowned. "But what's the point in delaying it for no reason?"

"Samira," Latifah said, a grin forming on her face, "it's not delaying prayer if you finish what you were doing before you pray."

Samira shrugged. "Well, you can pray late if you want. I'm praying now. My father said never play with your *salaat*."

"Play with your *salaat*?" Maryam laughed. "Samira, you really need to study Islam and get your facts straight. We're not playing with *salaat* just because we're not freaking out about not praying as soon as it comes in."

Samira glowered at Maryam. "You *should* be freaking out. How do you know you won't keep delaying it until you're late for real?"

Latifah sighed and pulled herself to her feet. "Samira's right. It's better to pray *salaat* now."

"In the Sunnah," Maryam said, standing herself, but her expression conveyed annoyance, "it's better to finish what you're doing so you can concentrate properly."

"But maybe that's just for breaking fast in Ramadan," Latifah said, wrapping her *khimaar* around her head.

"Why wouldn't it count for other things too?" Maryam put on her hijab then tucked an edge of the fabric under her chin to secure it.

"Oh, let's just pray," Samira said, exhaustion in her tone as she smoothed out the surface of her prayer garment with the palms of her hands. "Prayer is the wall between you and all evil. That's what my father says. I sure don't want evil any closer to me than it is already."

"Oh please," Maryam said, rolling her eyes. "It takes more than prayer to stay away from evil."

Latifah grinned and nodded. "But you can't deny prayer's a good start."

Samira nodded as they lined up next to each other, Maryam in the middle. "You don't have a chance without prayer," Samira said. "No matter what else you do." She smiled. "That's what my dad always says."

As it was obvious that Samira missed her father a great deal, Maryam and Latifah couldn't keep from smiling too.

* * *

"You first," Samira said, nodding her head to Latifah.

"Why me?" Latifah said, chuckling. "My life is boring."

"Liar," Samira said. "You beat boys in basketball."

Maryam's eyes widened as she looked at Latifah, gently yanking her friend's hand that she still held. "You play basketball with *boys*?"

Latifah sucked her teeth and rolled her eyes. "It's called gym class, Maryam. I didn't join the NBA."

"In hijab?"

Latifah creased her forehead as she met Maryam's wide stare. "Of course. What kind of Muslim do you think I am?"

"Her mom made this cool outfit." Samira's smile spread on her face. "It's a long sleeve shirt that goes to her knees, and it has matching gym pants."

"Really?" Maryam grinned. "That's so cool."

"It looks like a cheap *shawar khameez* if you ask me," Latifah said with a shrug.

"It does not," Samira said. "It looks like a proper gym uniform, except better. It matches the school colors and everything."

"Well, if that was my heart-to-heart," Latifah said, "you sure stole it."

"Sorry." Samira giggled as she brought a hand to her mouth, letting go of Latifah's hand.

"Okay, I got one," Latifah said.

The girls released each other's hands, and Maryam and Samira leaned forward, eager smiles on their faces.

"A boy asked for my phone number."

"What? No *way*." Samira eyed Latifah skeptically, but a hint of a smile was still on her face.

Maryam was speechless with a hand cupped over her mouth.

"Did you give it to him?" Samira asked.

Latifah playfully slapped Samira on the thigh and narrowed her eyes. "Do you think I want my parents on trial for murder?"

"Oh come on, Latifah," Samira said, laughing. "I don't think they'd kill him."

"Yeah, I know." Latifah sucked her teeth. "They'd kill *me*."

The girls exploded in laughter.

"Your turn," Samira called out, looking at Maryam.

"Me?" Maryam wore a look of surprise. "I go to Muslim school."

"And…?" Latifah fluttered her eyes sarcastically.

Maryam lifted a shoulder in a shrug. "Nothing interesting happens there."

"Like I believe that," Latifah said. "I remember seventh grade. They were up to all sorts of stuff."

"But this is high school."

"So?"

"So it's different."

Latifah started to say something but withheld, sensing that Maryam felt left out.

"Okay, then I'll go," Samira said, grinning.

"Okay." Latifah smiled eagerly.

"I think my mom is getting married again."

"Really...?" Latifah said, an uncertain expression on her face.

Samira nodded, obviously proud of the news.

"To who?" Latifah asked.

"I don't know."

"Then...how do you know she's getting married?"

"I hear her talking to someone on the phone." There was a sparkle in Samira's eye.

"What if it's not a man?" Latifah asked, hating to ask the obvious. She just didn't want to see Samira hurt.

"It's a man." Samira nodded emphatically. "I can tell by the way she talks."

"What about her *wali*?" Maryam furrowed her brows. "I mean, isn't it *haraam* to talk to a guy like that?"

Latifah turned to Maryam, scolding her with widening eyes.

"I'm serious," Maryam said, raising her voice defensively. "My dad says it's like doing *zina* for a man and woman to talk alone."

"Maryam." Latifah's tone conveyed exhaustion and thinning patience. "I really think you need to study Islam from someone other than your dad. No offense."

Maryam contorted her face. "What's that supposed to mean?"

"It means your dad's not the prophet, okay? My parents talked on the phone before they got married."

"But they weren't Muslim."

"Yes they were."

"But they didn't know about Islam yet."

"Yeah, you're probably right." A hint of sarcasm was in Latifah's voice. "They didn't know cultural Islam yet."

"My mom says *Americans* are the ones who follow cultural Islam." Maryam crossed her arms, offended.

Samira groaned aloud. "I can totally see her saying something like that."

"What?" Maryam glared at Samira.

Samira raised her palms in defense. "Hey, I'm just being honest. Your mom thinks she's a know-it-all."

"How dare you talk about my mother like that."

"How dare you talk about *our* mothers," Samira said.

"Latifah started it." Maryam's cheeks flushed. "How come she gets to talk bad about Desis and I can't talk bad about Americans?"

"I didn't hear her say anything about Desis," Samira said.

"She didn't have to. That's what she meant."

"No she didn't."

"Yes I did." Latifah's voice was devoid of energy.

Samira looked shell-shocked as she met Latifah's gaze.

"But I didn't mean only Desis. I meant all foreign Muslims."

"Foreign Muslims?" Maryam grunted. "Ummi says saying 'foreign' is impolite."

"Immigrant then. Whatever." Latifah rolled her eyes, shaking her head. "Same difference to me."

"Can you two please stop it?" Samira said, raising her voice.

Samira sighed. "Like Latifah said, maybe it's not even a man my mom's talking to."

An awkward silence followed. Latifah and Maryam were unsure what to say.

Samira's eyes grew sad. "I was just hoping it was my dad calling to take us back."

***

That night Basma and Joanne sat drinking tea with Latifah's mother in the living room of Basma's home. They had finished eating dinner a half hour before. Joanne and Rafiqah still wore their head covers though the men were at the masjid and were not due back for at least another hour.

"I'm sorry for all I put you through," Basma said. She sat on the loveseat across from where the two women sat on the couch. A sad smile lingered on her face as she met Joanne's gaze.

Joanne waved her hand dismissively. "I'm just glad you got up the nerve to make amends." She chuckled. "I'm a bit too headstrong for make-ups."

"Well, if you're stubborn when it comes to apologies," Rafiqah said with a grin, "you certainly are warmhearted in accepting them, *maashaAllah*."

Joanne smirked. "You don't know me well yet. You'll eat those words one day."

Rafiqah laughed lightly. "I doubt it."

Rafiqah took a sip of tea. "What was it you two were fighting about anyway?"

Joanne rolled her eyes to the ceiling as laughter escaped her throat. "Oh don't remind us."

A sad smile lingered on Basma's face. "It was my fault. I was being overly judgmental of Joanne's parenting."

"Shame on you." Grinning, Rafiqah reached forward to set her teacup on the saucer of the floor table. "I thought you were too sensible for that."

"I thought I was too," Basma said. "But I think that was the problem."

"You had a right to be judgmental," Joanne said. "I'm not the best mother in the world."

Rafiqah's eyebrows shot up. "Woe... Now don't go all pity-party on me. I don't think there's a such thing as a 'best mother,' if you ask me. We all walk on dirt, not water."

"True," Joanne said. "But some of us walk *in* dirt, not just on it."

"And if you're Muslim," Rafiqah said, "that dirt is washed away at every prayer."

"*InshaaAllah*," Basma added.

Rafiqah nodded. "*InshaaAllah*."

They were quiet for some time, and the distant sound of laughter came from upstairs where the girls were.

"Samira told me about the Muslim gym suit you made for Latifah."

"Oh, that?" The sides of Rafiqah's mouth creased in a smile. "You'd think I was asking to reinstate the draft, all they put me through to let her wear it."

Rafiqah looked over at Joanne. "What does Samira wear for gym?"

Joanne laughed. "Pants under the school shorts and a long sleeve shirt under the T-shirt."

"*MaashaAllah*, that's good," Rafiqah said.

"Maryam said your girls have a Muslim teacher," Basma said. "Is that true?"

Joanne nodded. "Yes, for U.S. history. He's from Pakistan."

Rafiqah chuckled. "He is indeed. The Desi club, that's what Latifah calls it. But she says he has a master's in Black history." Rafiqah shook her head, smiling. "The way Latifah tells it, he's a Pakistani Malcolm X."

Basma grinned. "*That* would be interesting."

"Well, I think she meant Malik El-Shabbaz," Rafiqah said, "not the Nation of Islam part."

A brief silence followed.

"Latifah doesn't mind wearing hijab and *jilbaab* to public school?" Joanne asked. Her eyes reflected intense interest as she looked at Rafiqah.

"I guess there's only one real answer to that," Rafiqah said. She reached for her teacup and took a sip but didn't say anything further.

"What's that?" Joanne asked after several seconds passed.

Rafiqah leaned forward until her elbows rested on her knees as she cradled the teacup with both hands. "I don't know."

"I can't imagine any teenager liking it," Basma said.

"Samira likes wearing hijab to school," Joanne said.

Basma gathered her eyebrows. "Really? *MaashaAllah.*"

"Well," Joanne clarified, "I don't have to force her to."

Rafiqah nodded. "Same here. *MaashaAllah.* Latifah's never given us any heat about it. Even when she was called rag head some years ago."

Basma rolled her eyes. "Maryam never got over being called that."

"Maryam used to go to public school?" Joanne sounded genuinely surprised.

Basma met Joanne's gaze with her brows furrowed. "Yes, in elementary school. You didn't know that?"

Joanne shook her head, smiling. "No. And I admit I'm quite surprised."

"Why?" Rafiqah asked.

Joanne shrugged. "I suppose I think of Basma as this perfect Muslim. I never expected her to put her daughter around non-Muslims."

Rafiqah chuckled. "Lord knows where you get your ideas. You should've given me a call. I've known Basma for years." She smiled at Basma. "I'll be the first to tell you she's far from perfect."

Basma shook her head, grinning. "Thanks."

"I'm just keeping it real."

"Well, at least I'm not the only imperfect Muslim here," Joanne said.

"Show me a perfect Muslim," Rafiqah said, "and you've met the *only* perfect Muslim that exists."

"But there has to be some measuring stick, you know?" Joanne said. "I mean, it's obvious some Muslims are better parents than others."

"Based on what?" Curiosity was in Rafiqah's tone.

Joanne shrugged. "I don't know... Maybe T.V., movies, music...stuff like that."

"Okay," Rafiqah said, "I admit I'm not a big fan of T.V. or movies, and we definitely don't do music. But really, I think parenting is much deeper than that."

"True," Joanne said with a nod. "But what about limits? Take the internet for examp—"

"Woe..." Humor was in Basma's voice. "I thought that topic was off limits."

Rafiqah creased her forehead as she looked at Basma. "Why? That's the perfect example."

Rafiqah turned back to Joanne. "I think we all have to set limits. But in the end, it boils down to knowing your child's strengths and weaknesses."

Joanne sat up straighter and nodded emphatically, a triumphant smile spreading on her face. "I totally agree. That was my point all along."

Rafiqah narrowed her eyes. "All along?"

"With the argument with Basma."

"Oh..." Rafiqah leaned back into couch and took a sip of tea, clearly not wanting to broach the subject.

"What's your opinion about internet in your house?" Joanne was looking at Rafiqah.

Rafiqah drew in deep breath. "Well... I admit I'm a little old-fashioned when it comes to the World Wide Web. I think it's more dangerous than T.V."

"Oh my God." Joanne laughed in relief. "That's exactly how I feel."

"But I think it's a necessary evil," Rafiqah said. "Everything's online today. Job postings, school applications, and even homework."

Joanne groaned. "Don't you hate that? Schools asking kids to go on YouTube for a school project?"

Rafiqah shook her head, agreeing. "That's certifiable mental illness in my opinion. Any time a teacher comes up with something like that, I'm at the school immediately, trust me."

"But YouTube is no different than Google," Basma said.

"Yeah?" Rafiqah huffed. "Do a search on YouTube then do the same on Google, and tell me if the same things come up."

"Does Latifah have internet in her room?" Joanne asked.

"Internet in her *room*?" Rafiqah rolled her eyes and grunted. "She doesn't even have a computer or a cell phone to call her own. We share. *Every*thing."

Basma shook her head as a grin lingered on her face. "Now I consider *that* overprotective."

Rafiqah lifted a shoulder in a shrug. "Consider it what you want. I call it common sense."

"And what exactly do you think you're protecting Latifah from?" Basma's tone conveyed amusement.

"I'm not sure I'm protecting her from anything, to tell you the truth." Rafiqah set her teacup down again. "It's me I'm trying to protect."

"You?" Basma laughed. "From what?"

"From sharing responsibility in any stupid choices she makes."

"Aren't you being a bit cynical?" Basma asked. "Assuming the worst?"

"Honey," Rafiqah said, humored, "sometimes I worry about you. Don't you know that *all* teens do stupid things at times?"

"Not necessarily."

"'All of the children of Adam sin,'" Rafiqah said. "Sound familiar?"

"That's a hadith, right?" Joanne asked.

Rafiqah nodded. "Sure is. A famous one too."

"But it doesn't say all *teens* sin," Basma said. "I think it's talking about adults."

Rafiqah raised an eyebrow. "I don't follow you."

"Some people die in childhood, correct?"

"Mm. Hm."

"Did they sin before they died?"

Rafiqah relaxed her expression and shrugged. "I see your point."

"But aren't teens adults in Islam?" Joanne said.

"Most are actually," Rafiqah said, nodding.

"*Young* adults," Basma said. "Still on their *fitrah* if they're Muslim."

Rafiqah raised her index finger. "Still *close* to their fitrah."

"My point is, it's about teaching them right from wrong," Basma said. "Being overprotective won't help."

"Look who's talking." Rafiqah laughed. "No T.V., no movies, not even animated pictures."

"Really?" Joanne's eyes grew large as she looked at Basma.

"Wait a minute," Basma said. "Now you're talking about violating Allah's laws. I didn't make those rules."

"Lord have mercy." Rafiqah rolled her eyes. "Tell me you didn't just say *Allah* forbids T.V. and movies."

"But not internet?" Joanne's eyes reflected amusement.

Basma shrugged her shoulders. "That's what I believe."

"Then you should believe the internet is forbidden too," Rafiqah said. "It has T.V., movies, *and* music all wrapped in one. And don't forget porn."

"Oh please." Basma chuckled. "I've never heard of a girl addicted to that."

"But you've heard of a teenage boy, huh?" Rafiqah asked. "That proves teens are not as pure as you think."

"Maybe boys aren't," Basma said.

"You really think Maryam isn't tempted to go beyond Google dot com, Wikipedia or Islamic sites when she's online?" Rafiqah's eyes conveyed amused disbelief.

"Maryam knows nothing about chat rooms and stuff like that," Basma said. "And even if she did, she's too innocent to even care about talking to boys or looking at *haraam, maashaAllah*."

"Well, if you're going to walk around wearing blinders, *ukhti*," Rafiqah said, sighing, "then you shouldn't wear them when other people's children are in your care."

Basma looked from Joanne to Rafiqah, her forehead creased, a grin lingering on her face. "Wait, was this some sort of sneak attack or something?"

"What do you mean?" Joanne asked.

"I just find it highly coincidental that Rafiqah's saying the same thing you were saying a few months ago."

"Basma," Rafiqah said, laughter in her voice. "I have no idea what went on between you and Joanne. But let me remind you, I'm from New York. If I see something that I think needs fixing, I'm not going to hide behind a sneak attack. I'll tell you what it is, point blank. Or I'll pray for you." A smile lingered on her face. "Or both."

***

"Thanks so much for that." Joanne said. It was late that night, and Joanne and Rafiqah stood on the sidewalk near where Hamid's car was parked behind Joanne's in front of Basma's house. Hamid and Faris were finishing a conversation under a glowing lamp on the front porch, and the girls stood just inside the house beyond the front door finishing a conversation of their own.

Rafiqah laughed, shaking her head. "Though I have no idea what you're so thankful about, you're welcome."

"For explaining everything so well, *maashaAllah.* I could never find the right words when Basma and I talked."

"Then you should thank Allah because it certainly wasn't my intention to add fuel to what happened between you two."

"I know, but I'm glad you said what you did."

Rafiqah smiled. "I love Basma like a sister, so I treat her like one too. I don't agree with everything she does, but I believe she has good intentions and is doing a wonderful job raising Maryam, *maashaAllah.* That's why I'm glad Latifah and Maryam are friends."

Joanne nodded. "And I'm glad Samira has Maryam and Latifah as friends."

Rafiqah reached out and squeezed Joanne's shoulder. "But don't beat yourself up about where you are with your Islam. You have to have a stronger personality if you're going to survive in a multicultural community."

Joanne averted her gaze as she was immediately reminded of her failed marriage. Maybe that had been her problem. Her mother had always said she would get hurt if she didn't "get some backbone."

"I know you know this from your travel and everything," Rafiqah said, "but when you're faced with so many different cultures and ideas, sometimes all you can do is stick to what your gut tells you is right."

"My mom always used to say that…"

"Well, she was right.

"And I don't think you should budge on your internet position," Rafiqah said thoughtfully. "I really think Basma's living in her own world when it comes to Maryam's innocence."

Joanne's forehead creased in deep concern. "Really?"

"Not like that." Rafiqah shook her head. "*MaashaAllah*, Maryam's a good girl, one of the best I know. But she's growing up, and I think Basma is making a big mistake by leaving her to her own devices."

Joanne nodded. "That's what I was thinking."

"Just make sure you let Basma know your limits. But personally," Rafiqah said, "I don't feel comfortable with Latifah coming over too often."

"Because of the internet?" Joanne looked surprised.

"Because of the internet *unsupervised*."

Joanne drew in a deep breath and exhaled. "That's what I was worried about before. But, *alhamdulillaah*, Basma promised me I don't have to worry about that anymore."

Rafiqah raised her eyebrows in surprise. "Really? Well… I hope you're right."

"You think I have cause to worry?"

Rafiqah chuckled and shook her head. "I'm not the best person to answer that. I always think parents have cause to worry. Latifah rarely comes here without me."

Joanne looked surprised. "Really? So you think…?"

"No, no, no." Rafiqah lifted a palm. "I don't mean to say I don't trust Basma. I just know what happens when parents think their children are angels. Call me cynical, but as innocent as Maryam is, *maashaAllah*, I don't see her any differently than I do the average teenager. Her innocence comes mostly from her parents, not her. And that's not necessarily a bad thing. I think the same about Latifah."

Rafiqah shook her head. "But the true test comes when our children make their own choices. What worries me is that Basma's blind trust of Maryam is premature. We have to teach our children responsibility. We can't just assume they already have it."

The sound of commotion and laughter prompted Rafiqah and Joanne to look toward the house. Hamid was making his way down the driveway as their daughters, still chatting, were steps behind.

"We'll be in touch, *inshaaAllah*," Rafiqah said.

"I'd like that."

"*As-salaaamu'alaikum.* Have a good night."

"*Wa'alaiku-mussalaam.* You too."

6

Homework Help

"Oooooh," Samira cried between bursts of giggles. She lay on a pile of autumn leaves with her arms stretched high above her head. She moved her arms and legs like scissors, the leaves crunching beneath her. "I can't wait till winter."

Latifah picked up a handful of leaves and dropped them on her friend as Samira squeezed her eyes shut in the afternoon sun.

"You'd freeze to death if this was snow," Latifah said with a laugh. "And you couldn't pay me to get buried in that stuff."

Samira fluttered her eyes open, a smile lingering on her face as she sat up. Leaves were sticking to her white pull-on hijab, but she brushed away the leaves that covered her lower body. "Coward. You can't die in the snow unless you faint or something."

"Well, you can get frostbite."

"Only if you stay out too long."

"And if you lie down like an idiot," Latifah said, rolling her eyes, "how would you even know what's 'too long'?"

A flash and a clicking sound prompted Samira and Latifah to look behind them.

"Got you," Rafiqah said, holding up a camera triumphantly.

The girls laughed.

"Why didn't Maryam come?" Samira said after Latifah's mother had retreated back to the park bench where Joanne was sitting drinking from a thermos and smiling at them after she witnessed Rafiqah steal a picture.

Latifah sat down on the leaves next to Samira. She squinted her eyes in the distance. "She has some homework due tomorrow."

Samira wrinkled her nose. "During vacation? That sucks."

"She goes to Muslim school, remember? They don't get Thanksgiving break."

"Oh yeah. I forgot about that. That's how it was in Saudi Arabia."

There was a brief pause.

"Did you start your research paper yet?" Latifah asked, looking at Samira.

"For history, you mean?"

"Yeah."

Samira groaned. "I'm still waiting for my mom to take me to the library."

"The library?" Latifah laughed. "Girl, I'm taking everything off line. He said three sources, but he didn't say they couldn't come from the internet."

Samira was quiet momentarily. "I don't have internet at home."

"Oh yeah. I forgot." Latifah's tone held a hint of sadness.

"I think it'll take me forever to finish this stupid essay."

"Not necessarily." Latifah's tone was optimistic. "The library has loads of books on the Great Depression."

"Uff," Samira said. "Just thinking about going there puts *me* in a great depression."

Latifah laughed. "Girl, you're so silly. I like going to the library."

"For schoolwork?"

"Okay, not for school. But I do like going."

"Isn't visiting a library like totally outdated?" Samira rolled her eyes. "This is the twenty first century. Libraries aren't buildings anymore. They're dot coms."

"Ask your mom if you can just come over my house then," Latifah said. "Our computer is in the living room, and my mom or dad is always there when we use it."

Samira crunched some leaves in her hand, her eyes growing distant. "Maybe."

"Why not? It'll be cool if we can help each other."

"Doesn't Mr. Butt call that cheating?"

Latifah shook her head, grinning. "Sharing internet? How is that plagiarism?"

"The way he talked, you'd think it's plagiarizing to even ask someone to edit your essay."

Latifah nodding, smiling. "I think he's just trying to scare us. A lot of students have other people write their essays."

A smirk formed on Samira's face. "Now, *that's* an idea."

"*Samira.*" Latifah glared at her friend playfully.

"Let's take some pictures," Samira said, grinning suddenly. She jumped to her feet then stretched out a hand toward Latifah. "Then we can save them on your computer for a memory book."

Latifah accepted Samira's hand, and Samira pulled her forward. They dusted off their clothes and Latifah picked the stray leaves from Samira's hijab before they walked to where their mothers were sitting, engrossed in conversation.

***

Arms folded in impatience, Maryam stood over Samira's shoulder as Samira surfed the net for sources for her history homework.

"Can you please hurry up?" Maryam groaned. "You said you'd be real quick."

"Can you calm down for God's sake? I'm almost done. I just need one more source."

"You said that fifteen minutes ago."

Samira turned sharply and met Maryam's annoyed gaze. "You can stop hovering over me."

Maryam bit her lower lip, her arms loosening at her chest as she tried to decide if she should leave Samira alone.

"My mom might come in," Maryam said.

Samira shrugged then turned back to the screen, clicking the mouse with her forefinger. "Let her. I'm not doing anything wrong."

"Why don't you just use the books you got from the library?"

"I already told you. I don't understand anything they're saying. Plus my paper's due Monday." Samira turned and met Maryam's gaze, this time her eyes demanding that Maryam back away.

Maryam rolled her eyes and gave in. She dragged herself to her bed and plopped down on the bedspread. She picked up a book that was face down on her pillow and tucked one leg under her, but her eyes did not leave Samira.

"I wish you would've just used Latifah's computer."

"Dummy," Samira said, eagerly tapping away at the keyboard, her eyes jumping back and forth from the monitor to her fingers, "I already told you my mom said no."

"And you want *me* to help you disobey your mother?"

Samira rolled her eyes as she dragged the mouse to highlight something on the screen and copied it to a document. "I wish you'd get off your soapbox. Like you *always* do what your parents say."

Maryam glared at the back of Samira's head. "I do."

Samira grunted laughter. "Yeah right. And I'm Jessica Simpson."

"I'm not lying."

"I believe you."

"Then why are you accusing me of disobeying my parents?"

"Because I know nobody's perfect, Dummy."

"I didn't say I was perfect."

"You act like you are."

"And so do you."

Samira glanced over her shoulder, a smirk on her face. "Now, that's something I've never claimed."

"Whatever."

"Yeah, whatever." Samira turned back to the computer.

"Done," Samira said after a few minutes passed. She stood and leaned forward to press the mouse one final time. A second later the printer hummed to life, buzzing and clicking as it spit out the papers.

Maryam jumped to her feet, exhaling a sigh of relief. "Finally."

She hurried to the computer and slid into her desk chair, her eyes on the monitor as she eagerly closed all the browser windows.

Samira removed the papers from the printer and tapped the stack on the flat of the desk. "Thanks, Maryam," she said as she lifted the straightened papers and stapled them. "You're a lifesaver."

Maryam's index finger halted on the mouse before she closed the last browser window. She drew her eyebrows together as she skimmed the unfamiliar site.

"Samira," she said slowly, "what's this?"

Samira was kneeling and stuffing the stapled papers into a folder in her backpack. "What?"

"This," Maryam said, turning to Samira and pointing to the screen.

Samira creased her forehead as she zipped her bag closed, narrowing her eyes to see the screen better. She stood and walked over to the computer.

"Oh." Samira grinned as she brought a hand to her mouth. "I forgot to sign out of Facebook."

Maryam blinked repeatedly. "You opened a Facebook account in my room? I thought you were doing homework."

"No, Dummy." Samira reached over Maryam's shoulder, taking the mouse from her to sign out. "I opened it in Saudi Arabia."

"Does your mom know about this?"

Samira rolled her eyes as she walked over to where her backpack lay on the floor. She sat down on the carpet, her body facing Maryam.

"Heart-to-heart time." Samira patted the ground in front of her.

"No it's not," Maryam said. "I don't feel like any stupid Friendship Style right now."

Samira shrugged. "Fine, then I won't answer any of your questions."

"Oh yes you will."

"Like a said, it's either heart-to-heart or my lips are sealed."

Maryam turned to the screen and clicked the small "x" in the corner of the sign-in screen for Facebook. "I swear I hate you."

"Don't swear, Maryam." Samira wagged a finger playfully. "It's not becoming of you."

"*You're* not becoming of me."

Maryam folded her arms as she sat down across from Samira.

"Give me your hands."

Maryam clinched her teeth as she reluctantly accepted. The warmth of Samira's palms on hers calmed her somewhat.

"Now close your eyes."

"Samira," Maryam said, contorting her face and pulling her hands away. Tears stung the back of her lids. "I can't."

Maryam pressed her fists against the carpet to push herself to a standing position. She shook her head. "You lied to me."

"I didn't lie to you, Maryam."

"You did too."

"I didn't."

"Then why were you on Facebook when you said you were doing history homework?"

"Because I *was* doing history homework, Dummy. I just wasn't *only* doing history homework."

Maryam's weight fell against the bed as she dropped herself on its edge, her arms folded in a pout. She kept shaking her head.

"You're never using my internet again," Maryam said. "Ever."

* * *

Late Monday morning Rafiqah pulled her car into a parking space at the public school that Latifah and Samira attended. She put the car in park and shut off the engine before pulling her keys from the ignition. The keys jingled as she looped the key ring around a finger. She pressed a button to unlock her door then reached over to the passenger seat to retrieve the bulging manila folder that contained the medical records that the school had called an hour earlier to request.

Rafiqah opened the driver's side door and stepped into the cool early December air, shutting the door with a slight movement of her hip. She tucked the manila folder under her arm as she pressed a button on her key chain to lock the car door before making her way to the main entrance of the school.

The sound of distant laughter and playful cries inspired in Rafiqah an uncomfortable awareness of her appearance. She wondered how she would look through the scrutinizing eyes of teenagers and school staff. The thought left her feeling self-conscious and vulnerable in the charcoal grey *khimaar* and voluminous black *jilbaab* that she hadn't given a second's thought about wearing when she had thrown them on twenty minutes before. But now a bitter taste lingered in Rafiqah's mouth as she imagined being gawked at and heckled. At least she wasn't wearing the face veil she had favored years before.

It was the post 9-11 Islamophobia and the strained relationship with her Christian parents and family that had worn her thin until she removed the *niqaab*, and she actually felt relieved after taking it off. A year earlier there had been moments when she was crippled with shame and guilt about her choice, but she had gradually come to believe that as long as she lived in America, it was for the better.

Of course Basma repeatedly made it clear that she didn't approve. But between beating up her own self about the decision and enjoying a better though strained relationship with her family, Rafiqah stopped caring what people like Basma thought—about anything. Rafiqah had even surprised herself by privately disapproving of Basma's choice to continue to wear *niqaab*—and all black—in the current political climate. But Rafiqah didn't like harboring those thoughts. After all, Basma felt it was obligatory to cover the face, so she should.

Fortunately, the halls of the school were relatively empty when Rafiqah made her way down the corridor to the front office.

"May I help you?" The voice came from an African-American woman whose eyes exuded kindness as she smiled at Rafiqah from behind the front desk of the main office.

"I'm here to drop off my daughter's medical records," Rafiqah said, her formal tone sounding foreign to her ears. "Someone called to say some files were missing."

"Oh yes. That was me." The woman swiveled her chair to a computer behind her and typed in something on the keyboard, glancing at the monitor.

"You're the mother of Latifah Hamid Bilal?" the woman asked, glancing from the screen to Rafiqah.

"Yes."

The woman nodded. "We just need a doctor's verification that she doesn't have any health issues that we should be concerned about. Also, it looks like we're missing a few vaccination records."

Rafiqah removed the manila folder from under her arm then placed it on the desk. She rummaged through the papers until she found what she was looking for then handed some papers to the woman.

The woman accepted them and ran a finger over the top of the papers to skim the contents. She nodded approvingly. "Perfect. I'll just make a copy of these and have these back to you in a minute."

The woman walked over to the large copy machine in a corner of the office, and Rafiqah glanced around at the plaques, posters, and certificates hanging on the walls. The cozy atmosphere settled Rafiqah's heart though she hadn't admitted to herself that she was worried about Latifah.

"And we're done." The woman smiled as she handed the papers back to Rafiqah. "We'll call you if we need anything else."

"Thanks. I appreciate it."

Rafiqah shuffled the papers in the folder then closed it around the bundle. She started to leave then hesitated as a thought came to her.

"Excuse me, ma'am?"

The woman looked up from where she now sat in front of the computer. "Yes?"

"What's the procedure for meeting a teacher?"

"Teachers are required to meet with parents only if there is a prior appointment," the woman said. "But if they aren't in class, they may meet a parent without an appointment so long as it's arranged through the front office."

The woman creased her forehead. "Would you like to meet one of your daughter's teachers?"

"Yes... If that's okay."

"No problem," the woman said. "If it's a planning period or lunch break, I page them and they let me know if they agree to meet." She paused. "Who would you like to meet?"

"The U.S. history teacher for ninth grade."

The woman's face brightened. "Oh. Mr. Butt? He's one of the students' favorite."

"Really?" Rafiqah couldn't contain her feeling of pride. It was always refreshing to hear about a Muslim having a good reputation.

The woman laughed heartily. "Yes. But we think he has a head start on other teachers."

A smile lingered on Rafiqah's face, uncertain how to respond.

"His name," the woman said with a grin. "He uses it as the butt of jokes. No pun intended."

Rafiqah burst into laughter, and the woman smiled broadly, chuckling herself.

"I'll page him now."

***

"I'm glad you stopped by," Mr. Butt said as Rafiqah walked in step with him down the hall. A visitor's badge dangled from the cloth of the head cover at her neck. "Latifah has made quite an impression."

"Really?" Rafiqah's lips spread into a smile she was unable to restrain.

"Oh yes. She's smart, confident, athletic…"

"Athletic?" Rafiqah laughed. "Now that's something new."

"She's one of our favorite students." Mr. Butt turned the handle of a classroom door then pushed it open, stepping to the side as he held the door open. Rafiqah stepped inside and he followed her, halting his steps briefly to prop the door open with the stopper affixed to the bottom of the door.

"I'm sorry we're not using the meeting room," he said, pressing a light switch. The fluorescent lights buzzed then flickered, and brightness flooded the room.

"Have a seat," he said, gesturing toward the U-shape arrangement of chairs.

They both took a seat at a student's desk, leaving one desk between them.

"What's on your mind?" Concern was etched in Mr. Butt's tone.

"Oh nothing in particular," Rafiqah said. "It's just that Latifah goes on and on about you, so I wanted to meet you in person."

Mr. Butt smiled slightly, his restrained eyes suggesting that he was more cautious than flattered, and

86

Rafiqah could tell he was accustomed to hearing this sentiment from parents. She sensed his years of experience had taught him that student admiration was not always preferable.

"Well, I'm happy to have her." Mr. Butt's tone conveyed sincerity. "It's always heartwarming to meet Muslims who are proud of their faith, especially among the youth."

Rafiqah nodded, her thoughts drifting to some youth who had left Islam. "That's certainly the truth."

"And with her academic standing," Mr. Butt said, lifting his eyebrows, impressed, "I wouldn't be surprised if she's the class valedictorian come senior year."

Rafiqah jerked her head in surprise. "You think so?"

"Certainly."

Rafiqah breathed a sigh of relief. "I can't tell you how much better that makes me feel." She chuckled, shaking her head. "I was beginning to doubt that we made the right decision putting her in public school."

Mr. Butt nodded thoughtfully. "But I do have one concern, Mrs. Bilal."

Rafiqah drew her eyebrows together. "What's that?"

He scratched at the side of his thin beard and Rafiqah sensed he was trying to decide what to divulge.

"Basketball."

The lines in Rafiqah's forehead deepened. "I'm sorry, but I'm not following you."

Mr. Butt glanced at his wristwatch. "Look, I don't want to keep you. I know both of our schedules are pretty busy."

"Mr. Butt, please." Rafiqah's tone was of strained patience. "I have all day if it's for the sake of my daughter."

"Well..." He drew in a deep breath and exhaled. "From one Muslim parent to another, Mrs. Bilal, I'm concerned the sport is being used as an excuse to have physical contact with boys."

It took a few seconds for Rafiqah to register what he was saying. "But..." Her eyes reflected confusion. "...when does she play basketball? I didn't see it on her schedule."

"Gym class."

Rafiqah's face grew warm in mortification. "Well, why are girls and boys playing together? The school should keep them separate for contact sports."

Mr. Butt met Rafiqah's gaze as he rubbed his chin thoughtfully. His lips formed a thin line of disapproval. "It does keep them separate, Mrs. Bilal. It's Latifah who insists on bending the rules."

7

Caught

Latifah held her hands high in the air to block Kendrick's shot. Her knee-length gym shirt that her mother had made was tied in a thick knot at her waist. The loose fabric of the matching gym pants slightly hugged her hips, and sweat beaded at her hair line that was exposed because her scarf had slipped back during the game.

The physical education teacher used to ask Latifah to stay on the other side of the gymnasium where the girls were playing, but Kendrick would always wear the teacher down with his charismatic reasoning.

"We're not hurting anybody," he'd say, a pleading grin on his face.

"Fine," the teacher would say after going back and forth for several minutes. "But only after you both finish the workout I assigned."

"Thanks, Mrs. Bradford. God loves you."

"Oh shut up, Kendrick," the teacher would say playfully, shaking her head and grinning as she made her way back to the bleachers to watch the co-ed class, a whistle dangling from a cloth string around her neck.

"You look good today," Kendrick whispered to Latifah, his hands still poised in the air as he watched the ball swoosh through the net.

Latifah giggled as she went to retrieve it. "You say that every day," she called out as she caught the bouncing ball.

Kendrick's smirk spread as he jogged to where Latifah was dribbling the ball, her knees bent in preparation to shoot. He stood in front of her and spread his arms wide, taunting her with his eyes.

"You ain't going to make it," he teased.

She faked to the left then shot the ball to the right, his hand falling shy of blocking the ball.

Latifah watched anxiously as the ball hit the rim and rolled around it. A second later, it fell into the basket, yanking the netting back and forth before it bounced to the ground.

The sound of whistle a blowing halted Kendrick's steps to retrieve the ball.

"Man." He grunted as he turned to look at Mrs. Bradford near the bleachers. He playfully contorted his face, his arms stretched out, as if saying, *What's up with that?*

Latifah bent down to pick up the ball. As she stood holding it, she felt a strong arm wrap around her waist. "Woe..." she said, laughing as she was suspended in the air before Kendrick set her back down. "What's wrong with you?"

"Sorry," he said as they fell in step with the rest of the students heading toward the bleachers near the exit doors. "I just wanted to pick you up in class since I can't pick you up tonight."

Latifah rolled her eyes, a grin lingering on her face. "I told you I'm not allowed to date."

"Yes you did. But I ain't going to give up on you. You make my heart throb." He winked at her, and she shook her head, laughing.

"I bet you say that to all the girls."

"Nuh uh." He shook his head and eyed Latifah approvingly. "Because none of them look like you."

"All right you two," Mrs. Bradford said, her eyes smiling as she raised a hand above her head to let the class know she wanted their attention. "Quiet."

As Mrs. Bradford talked to the class about a winter sports day, Latifah stood next to Kendrick, her face warm in flattery, unable to process anything the teacher was saying. Kendrick grasped Latifah's hand and squeezed it, as if saying he wanted her to stay right where she was— by his side. Latifah was too shy to grip his hand in return, but she didn't ask him to let go. Because she didn't want him to.

***

Rafiqah stood as if in a trance in front of the entrance to the high school gymnasium. She could not rip her eyes away from the double doors that were affixed with glass windows that were transparent from the outside but reflective mirrors from inside.

"Mrs. Bilal?"

Rafiqah heard the deep voice of Mr. Butt, who stood feet behind her, his head bowed sadly and his arms folded as he waited for her to finish. But she didn't move. A numbness paralyzed her arms and legs.

"Mrs. Bilal?" This time the voice came from next to her, and in her peripheral vision, she could see Mr. Butt glance through the glass then frown. "I have a class now. We'll need to go."

Rafiqah's head moved forward in the beginning of a nod, and she somehow managed to turn away from the glass.

"Don't forget to sign out in the front office and return the visitor's pass," he said.

"Thank you," she said. But only her lips moved. No sound came out.

Awkward silence followed as Mr. Butt stood opposite her, his arms still folded, his mouth forming a thin line.

"I'm really sorry about this."

"I owe you an apology," Rafiqah managed to mutter. "I shouldn't have bothered you with this."

"Mrs. Bilal, I'm Muslim too." He sighed, shaking his head. "So I know this isn't cute or innocent like I'm sure Mrs. Bradford imagines it to be."

At the reminder of this all happening under adult supervision, Rafiqah tasted acrid bile rise to the back of her throat. She swallowed hard, fighting the urge to vomit right there.

Mr. Butt lifted his wrist and glanced at his watch. "We better go. The bell will ring soon, and we don't want them to find us out here."

It was those words that inspired life to return to Rafiqah's limbs, and she fell in step behind Mr. Butt as he retreated down the hall.

***

That Friday afternoon, Samira walked quietly up to where Maryam was engrossed in something on the computer screen. She stood a safe distance behind Maryam's shoulder as she watched Maryam type rhythmically on the keyboard.

After the day Maryam had caught Samira on Facebook, Maryam refused to speak to Samira or acknowledge her presence. Though Maryam previously did not log on to the internet when Samira visited, she started to surf the Web when Samira came over so that she could ignore her more easily.

"I thought you didn't chat with boys."

Maryam started. Eyes wide, she turned to find Samira looking at the computer screen. Maryam's cheeks colored and she immediately clicked the mouse, minimizing the window.

"That would've made a juicy heart-to-heart," Samira said with a grin.

Maryam slapped the desk as she turned to Samira. "I'm not chatting with boys."

"That looked like a chat to me."

"It's a Muslim site." Maryam tossed her head proudly. "Not Facebook."

"*I* don't chat with boys. Not even on Facebook." Samira smirked as she folded her arms over her chest. "But maybe it's Islamic to mix with boys when it's not Facebook?"

"I'm not mixing with boys." Maryam huffed then turned back to the screen, shutting down the computer.

"You're just chatting with them, huh?"

"That wasn't a boy." Maryam stood, pulling the book off the desk next to her. She walked over to her bed and sat down on the bedspread, folding her legs like a pretzel.

"Abdullah-eight-eight-eight?" Samira tossed her head back in laughter. "That sounds like a boy's screen name to me."

Maryam's cheeks were flushed as she looked up from her book. "I wasn't talking to him."

"So you're admitting that Abdullah isn't a girl?"

Maryam narrowed her eyes into slits. "Why don't you mind your business? I was asking a question about Islam."

"Yep…" Samira pursed her lips and snapped her fingers. "How could I ever imagine the saint would want to flirt?"

"Samira! How dare you."

Samira threw up her hands, palms facing Maryam. "But don't mind me. I'm sure your question was of the utmost urgency." She smiled mischievously. "So…when I just casually mention to my mom that you go online, I'll say you were getting a fatwa?"

Maryam's mouth fell open.

Samira wagged a finger. "Don't think I'd keep such an impeccable act of righteousness secret. The whole ummah should know that Maryam... No, wait—" Samira pressed her eyes shut and squeezed the bridge of her nose. "Yes, that's it!" Samira opened her eyes and brought her palms together. "That Muslimah-two-two-five wants to save them from sin and corruption."

"Look..." Maryam threw her book down as she met Samira's gaze, her voice casual. "I don't go even there all the time. I just wanted to ask a question."

"And I presume you got your answer?"

Maryam looked uncertain. "Well..."

Samira waved a hand about her head. "Don't worry about it. Who am I anyway? I'm not worth your time." A smile spread on her face, her eyes twinkling. "But I'm sure Abdullah-eight-eight-eight is."

"Samira, it's nothing like that, I swear."

"I believe you." Samira clasped her hands behind her back as she paced the room. "I totally believe you. Just like I know you *never* disobey your parents." A grin formed on her face. "Now, do you?"

Maryam sniffed. "My mom lets me go online anytime I want."

"I'm sure she does." Samira shrugged. "So I'm sure it won't surprise her when my mom tells her you chat with boys."

"And I'll tell *your* mom that you have Facebook!"

Samira laughed. "Well, news to you. My mom knows I have Facebook."

Maryam started to say something but stopped herself. "I don't believe you."

"Suit yourself. She knows. She found my Facebook page when we lived in Saudi."

Maryam just stared at Samira, unsure what to say.

"And I really don't care if she knows I used internet for homework. I might get in trouble, but—" Samira shrugged. "I'm sure she'll get over it since it was for school."

Samira regarded Maryam, a smile toying at her mouth as she folded her arms across her chest. "But you, my friend, have a lot of explaining to do about why you think it's totally okay to chat with boys."

***

The parking lot at the masjid that night was packed with cars. The speaker for the night's lecture was known for his charisma, humor, and moving recitation of Qur'an. Even Muslim youth crowded the halls as they made their way to the main prayer hall to find a place to sit.

Samira spotted Latifah just as Latifah was kneeling outside the female prayer entrance to remove her shoes.

"Latifah," Samira called out. She turned sideways to wedge herself between some women who were standing casually in the hall with their young children playing at their feet and their babies bawling so loudly that Samira could feel vibrations in her ears.

"Latifah!"

Latifah held her shoes mid-air as she looked behind her, her forehead creased.

Samira waved.

As their gazes met, Latifah broke into a wide grin and glanced down as she dropped her shoes on the floor and slipped them back on.

"Where have you been, stranger?" Latifah said. Samira smirked then grabbed Latifah's arm and guided her away from the crowd.

"I have to tell you something," Samira said.

Before Latifah could reply, Samira let go of Latifah's arm and pushed open one of the double exit doors that led to the masjid's playground.

"Come on," Samira said. "It won't be so noisy out here."

The rush of cold night air ripped through their head covers, causing the cloth to flap against their heads.

"Brrrr..." Latifah lifted her shoulders to shield her ears from the wind as she pushed her bare hands deep into the pockets of her coat. "It's freezing out here."

"It'll only be a second," Samira said as the door slammed closed behind them.

There was the distant sound of car engines stalling, car doors closing, and families chattering in the parking lot adjacent to the playground. The darkness outside was interrupted only by the street lamps blazing above the parked cars. A dim glow from the lamps lighted the area where the girls stood under an awning, feet from the double doors.

"You won't believe what I caught Maryam doing today," Samira said in a loud whisper, leaning toward Latifah's ear.

The faint smell of cigarette smoke drifted to where they stood, and it was then that they noticed the shadow of a man sitting about twenty yards from them on a park bench in the playground, a tiny red glow of a cigarette in his hand. At the slight commotion of the girls, he turned to see who was there, a blank expression on his face. Frowning, he returned his attention to the deep darkness beyond the park.

"Maryam?" Latifah laughed, rolling her eyes. "Girl, you brought me all the way out here for some stupid gossip?"

"It's not gossip. I'm telling the truth."

Latifah shivered as a cold breeze swept toward them. "What was Maryam doing? And it better be worth my fingers falling off because I can't feel them anymore."

"Talking to boys."

Latifah jerked her head toward Samira, her eyes widened. "You're lying."

"I swear. I was standing behind her, but she didn't see me."

"Where?"

"In her room."

Latifah's eyes grew so large that Samira feared that Latifah was having a heart attack.

"Boys? In her *room*?" Latifah narrowed her eyes. "How?"

Samira sucked her teeth and rolled her eyes upward as she realized why Latifah was so shocked. She laughed then slapped Latifah's shoulder playfully. "No, stupid. I mean on the computer."

Latifah slowly closed her eyes in relief, puffing out a breath of air as she brought a hand to her chest. "Thank God. I was about to pass out."

Samira laughed. "No way. I mean…." She wrinkled her nose. "Ewww! That's just…yuck."

"Anyway, how do you know she was talking to boys?"

"The screen name. It was Abdullah-eight-eight-eight."

"Are you serious?"

"She said it was a Muslim chat room and she was just asking a question." Samira twisted her lips to the side and crossed her arms, as if saying, *And you think I'm buying that?*

Latifah shrugged. "Maybe it was. I can't see Maryam chatting for no reason. It's not like her."

Samira put her hands on her hips. "Are you nuts? Everybody has a devil in them."

"I don't believe that."

"My mom says so all the time."

"I think she was joking, kiddo."

"No, I mean, like a real devil. A jinn."

"Oh now you're going superstitious on me."

"Oh, come on, Latifah. You know I'm saying the truth. It's in the Qur'an."

Latifah huffed. "Like I believe that."

"Hello, Latifah?" Samira said sarcastically. "Haven't you heard of a *qareen*?"

Latifah started to respond but stopped herself. "You mean like the…" Her hand went to her mouth. "Oh yeah. You're right. I forgot about the jinn that stays with us." She shuddered.

"Don't remind me," Latifah said. "I swear, I couldn't sleep for days when the Islamic studies teacher told us about that."

"So…" Samira said, returning to the subject of Maryam. "It isn't like Maryam has an angel with her and the rest of us have a devil."

"Okay," Latifah said, slipping her hand back into her coat pocket, "even if that's true. That doesn't make her a bad person." She shrugged. "If she says she was just asking a question, I think she was."

"So it's okay to talk online, you think?" Samira's tone was of heightened curiosity, as if considering this perspective for the first time.

Latifah lifted her shoulders to her ears again, shivering as wind blew in her face. "I don't see why not. It's about your intentions."

Samira's expression was thoughtful as she looked at Latifah. "Would you? I mean, talk online to boys?"

Latifah averted her gaze, and Samira sensed her friend was thinking about the basketball games. Though Samira wasn't in Latifah's physical education class, she'd heard enough from schoolmates to know that if any of the rumors were true, Latifah wasn't as innocent as Samira had initially imagined.

"I never have," Latifah said. Her eyes were looking out toward the playground, where the man was crushing a cigarette with his shoe. "But I guess I would if I wasn't talking about anything bad."

"I never have either," Samira said.

"What?" Latifah wore a smirk as she looked at Samira. "But you have Facebook."

"But I never added any boys."

Latifah looked genuinely surprised, and Samira felt a tinge of offense. Why did everybody think she was such a horrible person?

"I'm serious," Samira said. "Boys scare me."

Latifah laughed, but the sound was devoid of its usual heartiness. Samira sensed Latifah was feeling ashamed of herself again, and Samira wished she hadn't said anything to remind Latifah of school.

Latifah let out a long sigh, staring distantly into the shadows of the playground. "They scare me too."

8

Change

"Tell me, brothers and sisters..." the speaker said. His voice reverberated in the main prayer hall and from the intercoms in the masjid corridors. Men sat in rows shoulder to shoulder on the carpeted floor, as did the women in their section, and those who had come late sat in the hallways on carpet that had been rolled out to accommodate the massive crowd. "...how did you just spend the last twenty four hours?"

There was a brief pause, and the microphone screeched. "Don't worry," the speaker said with a chuckle. "I'm not going to ask you to tell me out loud. So you can be honest with yourself."

Uncomfortable laughter rippled through crowd. But seconds later, silence ensued, as the attendees sat reflecting on all they had done the previous day up till now.

"If I asked you to write it all down, put your name on it, and pass it to me, would you mind if I read it aloud?" the speaker said. "Then would you mind if I sent it to the tabloids, those shameful magazines that earn a living off of insulting people's dignity, ruining reputations, breaking apart marriages, and destroying the most innocent of lives?"

He was silent momentarily as the question took full meaning.

"Then tell me, brothers and sisters, why we do the same to ourselves? Why do we insult our dignity, ruin our reputations, break apart our marriages, and destroy the innocent beauty of the lives Allah gave us at birth?"

The speaker sought refuge in Allah and his voice rose as he recited from the *soorah* of Qu'ran entitled *Al-Hadeed*—The Iron.

Has not the time come for the hearts of those who believe to be affected by Allah's Reminder, and that which has been revealed of the truth? Lest they become like those who received the Scripture before and the term was prolonged so their hearts were hardened? And many of them were rebellious and disobedient.

After he translated the meaning in English, he asked, "Hasn't that time come, brothers and sisters?" He paused before saying, "Or are you waiting for the earth to cover your bodies as you lie alone in your grave? But then you won't have any choice but to answer aloud when you are commanded to tell how you spent the last hours of your life."

***

"And now you want us to just take her out the school?" Hamid shook his head as he poured himself a glass of orange juice in the kitchen early Saturday morning. Their children had not yet wakened after praying *Fajr* prayer at dawn.

Rafiqah sat at the kitchen table in front of a bowl of cereal she no longer had an appetite for. She stabbed at the softening flakes with a spoon, her thoughts sad and distant.

After the lecture the night before, Rafiqah had been unable to sleep. She kept waking intermittently, anxiety tightening her chest. The image of the knotted cloth at Latifah's waist and Latifah's bursts of laughter as the muscle-toned boy lifted her off the ground kept playing over in her mind. When Rafiqah finally drifted to sleep, she was tormented with a dream of the handsome boy coaxing Latifah into a kiss in a misty locker room as the darkness of night closed around them, the abandoned school building locked and chained from the outside.

"I remember you said the same thing when Latifah was in the Muslim school." Chair legs screeched against the tile floor as Hamid pulled out a chair for himself. His juice glass made a banging noise as he sat down and set it on the table. "And I distinctly remember disagreeing with you."

"I was wrong, Hamid. I realize that now."

Rafiqah was uncertain how much she should share with her husband. All she had told him was that the P.E. teacher was allowing some students to play co-ed sports and Latifah was participating. She knew that if she revealed the details of the meeting with Mr. Butt and what she had seen with her own eyes, Hamid would withdraw Latifah immediately and punish her severely. But that couldn't happen without Latifah learning that her parents knew what was happening. Rafiqah feared the humiliation of Latifah openly facing her sin would crush her daughter.

Rafiqah had been young once, and she recalled how traumatizing it had been when her parents berated her for a stupid mistake she had made. She was now almost forty years old, and she still had not recovered. Her parents had even brought up the incident a few years before when they scoffed at her "hypocrisy" in practicing Islam. It had felt like she was fifteen all over again, shrinking under the harsh judgment of parents who could not forget or forgive.

There was certainly divine wisdom in the prophetic instruction to cover a person's faults, and that was what Rafiqah intended to do for Latifah. Rafiqah would not take from Latifah what her parents had taken from her—a right to the human dignity and respect they demanded for themselves.

"You realize that now." Hamid grunted and shook his head as he repeated his wife's words. He lifted the glass he held then finished the juice in gulps. He set the empty glass on the table, a ring of orange reflecting on the bottom.

"What about all the psychological trauma you talked about?" Hamid said. "All the racist taunting from fellow Muslims that you said would scar her for life? That doesn't matter to you anymore?"

"It matters to me. It's just that I realize now that the trauma of public school could be worse."

Hamid threw his head back in amused laughter. "Oh doesn't that sound familiar?" He was looking at his wife now.

"Yes," Rafiqah said, unable to meet his gaze. "It's the reason you gave for saying we should keep her in Muslim school."

"Man, I tell you, Rafiqah. You really had me convinced. I kept thinking about all the post-traumatic stress Black people suffer, and what our parents went through fighting Jim Crow only to wish they could make separate-but-equal work."

"I don't know, Hamid. I still think Muslim school will leave scars, you know, with all the racism these immigrants bring from their cultures. But..." She breathed thoughtfully. "...I guess it's like they say. Damned if you do, damned if you don't. You know what I mean?"

He huffed in agreement, a smile lingering on his face. "Ain't that the truth."

"At Muslim school, I'm still worried about her psychological well being. But now..." She stirred the soggy cereal, lost in thought. "...I'm worried about her soul."

Hamid was quiet, his eyes squinted as he shook the empty glass. There was the sound of movement upstairs, likely one of the children waking up and preparing to come downstairs for breakfast.

"I'll think about it," he said finally.

Seconds passed in silence, and Hamid chuckled to himself. "I remember one thing my father always said. 'Son, women will drive you nuts with all their crazy feelings and what not, so you just have to be a man and do what you know is right. But don't trivialize the intuition of a good woman, son. I swear to God, sometimes I feel like it comes from the Lord himself.'"

* * *

"Now I hope you'll stop using that stupid Facebook," Maryam said. It was Saturday afternoon and Samira sat facing the monitor of Maryam's computer, Samira's hand poised on the mouse as Maryam guided her through the process of navigating the Muslim site.

"You have to click 'OK'," Maryam said, leaning forward and pointing to an icon on the screen.

"This is so cool," Samira said as she clicked the final approval button to open an account on the Muslim website that Maryam frequented.

Maryam rolled her eyes. "Yeah, but I wish you would've chosen a different screen name."

"What's wrong with Desi-girl-one-oh-one?" Samira turned her head slightly and met Maryam's gaze. "I like it."

"It just sounds so...worldly."

"Oh, stop it. Now you're sounding like your mother."

At the mention of her mother, Maryam felt a tinge of guilt for giving in to Samira's urging to let her use the computer.

"And between you and me, I couldn't care less if Samira surfs the net."

At the reminder of her mother's words, Maryam's anxiety lessened. Maryam would just make sure Samira stayed on Muslim sites. Then maybe Samira wouldn't care about posting pictures of herself on Facebook, even if she didn't have any boys as friends. Anyway, how could she be sure none of her friends' brothers saw the pictures?

But part of Maryam dreaded what her mother would think if she found out Samira was going online.

"That's the least of our worries." Her mother was right, Maryam thought to herself. There were thousands of worse things Samira could be doing. Sister Joanne would be better off asking her daughter to follow the Islamic rules about music and proper hijab.

9

Friction

"What made you decide to put Latifah back in Muslim school?" Basma asked.

It was a Sunday evening in mid-January, and Basma held a glass half-full of juice as she sat across from Joanne and Rafiqah on the Arab-style floor couch that lined the walls of the finished basement of Rafiqah's family townhouse. A mat covered with partly eaten food, chips, desserts, and condiments was at their feet. The luncheon that Rafiqah had hosted had ended an hour before, but she had told Basma and Joanne that they could stay longer if they liked.

"We prayed on it," Rafiqah said, "and Hamid and I decided Muslim school would bring the greater good *inshaaAllah.*"

"That's what I felt all along," Basma said. She took a sip from her juice, looking over the glass at Rafiqah. "Those public schools ruin our girls."

"You don't think they do the same for boys?" Joanne said. She balanced a paper plate of snacks and vegetables on her lap. Forehead creased, she regarded Basma as she lifted a potato chip then dabbed it in sour cream before bringing it to her mouth.

"Perhaps," Basma said. "But it's worse for girls."

"Why?" Rafiqah smiled. "Because boys don't leave any evidence?"

Joanne chuckled, bringing a hand to her mouth to cover the food she was still chewing.

"You can't deny girls have more to lose," Basma said.

"In what sense?" Rafiqah asked. "Culturally or spiritually?"

Basma sighed, shaking her head. "It always comes back to that, doesn't it? Our culture. You Americans have cultural baggage too."

Rafiqah raised her eyebrows. "I didn't mention any specific culture. I was speaking in general. Though I'm sure you know American culture is more Islamic as far as these issues are concerned."

Basma clicked her tongue. "You should never call American culture Islamic."

Joanne drew her eyebrows together as she stirred a carrot stick in the vegetable dip. "Why not?"

Exhaustion was in Basma's eyes as she looked at Joanne. "American culture is not compatible with Islam."

Joanne looked as if she was preparing to respond, but Rafiqah spoke first.

"I disagree."

Basma's eyes widened slightly. It was obvious she hadn't expected this remark to come from Rafiqah. "How can you disagree? You know as well as I do that America's laws are not based on Islam."

"And I don't expect them to be," Rafiqah said. "Laws and culture are two different things. Laws are always changing. Culture is more or less a constant."

Basma shook her head as she glanced at the glass in her hand. "Okay, but how is American culture more Islamic than Pakistani culture?"

"I didn't say it was. I said American culture is more Islamic when it comes to how it views boys and girls making mistakes."

"American culture is too permissive if you ask me," Basma said. "You all have no *hayaa'* in these matters."

Rafiqah fluttered her eyes in surprise, amusement on her face. "Excuse me? I think all humans have a sense of shame."

Basma shook her head. "Not most Americans."

"What?" Joanne was clearly offended.

"I'm speaking in general," Basma said. "Of course, those who become Muslim learn *hayaa'* from Islam."

"My parents were very strict Christians," Rafiqah said. "I wasn't even allowed to date until I was eighteen. And I had to be chaperoned by my parents."

"But that's rare," Basma said. "Most Americans let their children intermingle from childhood, and it doesn't stop at puberty. In fact, they encourage them to mix with the opposite sex."

Joanne laughed aloud. "Are you serious? That's not true at all."

"Believe what you want, Basma." The corners of Rafiqah's mouth creased in the beginning of a smile. "It's what you'll do anyway. But you're speaking of American TV culture. We're speaking of real life."

Joanne grunted agreement, shaking her head.

Basma frowned, clearly offended by Rafiqah's words, but she didn't respond.

"My point is that American culture views sins similar to how Islam views sins," Rafiqah said. "But most immigrant Muslim cultures have double standards that favor boys."

"For example?" Basma asked.

"In America, a girl's life isn't over just because she committed a sin," Rafiqah said.

"That's because sin is looked at as something praiseworthy in your culture," Basma said.

Rafiqah drew in a deep breath and exhaled, a smile lingering on her face. "I find it quite ironic that you seem to know more about our culture than we do."

"Maybe that's because I'm on the outside looking in," Basma said. "It's easier to be objective that way."

"Or more judgmental," Rafiqah said, shaking her head.

"If the culture is as bad as you say," Joanne said, looking at Basma, "then why did you leave your country and get American citizenship?"

"That's beside the point," Basma said.

"No," Rafiqah said. "I think it's the crux of the issue here. You say there's nothing Islamic about this culture, yet you left Pakistan just to get American passports."

"Life is difficult in our countries," Basma said with a frown. "That's something you'll never understand."

"So you came to an un-Islamic environment to have an easier life?" Rafiqah huffed, a smirk on her face. "That sounds totally Islamic."

"Is something wrong with Muslims wanting a better life?" Basma said.

"No," Rafiqah said. "I'd love a better life myself. I'm just saying you yourself don't believe what you're saying. Otherwise you couldn't live here. It would be *haraam*."

***

"*Who* is that?" A week later, Maryam stood with her hands on her hips, feet behind where Samira was on the computer.

"Come look!" Samira giggled, no shame traceable in her voice.

Maryam closed her eyelids slowly. She rolled her eyes to the ceiling as she dragged herself to where Samira was on the computer. *O Allah!* I hope this is just some stupid website Samira found by accident.

"Isn't he cute?" Samira squealed.

As shocking as the words were to Maryam's ears, Maryam actually looked—closely.

"Yeah... he is," Maryam said, distracted momentarily from her own offense.

Maryam immediately brought a hand to her mouth. Oh my God. *What did I just say?*

"Samira…" Maryam's voice was more cautious this time. "…is this the brother you were arguing with on the Muslim site?"

Samira shot Maryam a confused glance and waved her hand dismissively. "No. This," she said, "is Jason."

The name stung Maryam's ears until her whole head became enflamed. Jason wasn't a Muslim name.

Then again… Neither was Joanne.

Maybe he converted?

"Um…" Maryam said. "…is he Muslim?"

Samira sucked her teeth and rolled her eyes. "Of course not."

Maryam felt her legs go weak, but she gripped the back of the desk chair until the dizziness passed. There was a sudden knotting in her head that gave way to throbbing at her temples.

"Samira," Maryam managed to murmur as her throat went dry.

"Yeah?"

"We need to have a heart-to-heart."

"Okay." Samira's voice was chipper as she continued maneuvering the mouse and looking at the screen.

"*Now.*"

Samira winced, turning to look at Maryam, her eyes scolding. She turned back to the screen. "Give me a minute."

Maryam reached down and clicked the power switch. There was a slight popping sound and a faint whine from the monitor and process unit.

"No," Maryam said after Samira met her gaze wide eyed. "I won't wait. We need to talk *now.*"

"Okay already." Samira slapped her palms on the desk as she stood.

10

Heart-to-Heart

"Don't you think you should tell her mom?" Latifah said. She removed the wax paper from her rye-bread sandwich that was layered with slices of meat, lettuce, tomatoes and cheese. She sat next to Maryam at the far end of a lunch table, apart from the other girls who were eating in the cafeteria of the Muslim school.

Latifah shook her head, unable to figure out how in just a matter of weeks Samira went from boys scaring her to chatting with a non-Muslim guy online.

Then again... Latifah herself was guilty of worse.

"How?" Maryam drew in a deep breath and exhaled as she opened a sealed container of *biryani* her mother had packed for her. "My mom will kill me."

"Why would your mother blame you?" Latifah said. "You're not the one chatting with boys."

Just then, Latifah was reminded of the conversation about Maryam that she and Samira had had outside the masjid the night of the lecture.

"Anyway, how do you know she was talking to boys?" Latifah had asked Samira.

"The screen name. It was Abdullah-eight-eight-eight."

Maryam averted her gaze and rummaged through her lunch box in search of something.

Was it possible that Maryam had done more than just ask an Islamic question?

Maryam pulled out a fork and began eating in silence, her eyes still avoiding Latifah's gaze.

Latifah's heart sank. She remembered the wrenching guilt she had suffered after each gym class each day...only to eagerly look forward to the next one.

O Allah. Now Maryam too?

"Everybody has a devil in them" Samira had said. Latifah had no idea if the *qareen* was actually inside each person. But, either way, Latifah was beginning to realize that staying away from sin was much more complicated than she had imagined it to be.

"Maybe it's not a big deal," Maryam said. She shrugged. "Samira's talking to him about Islam."

Latifah took a bite of her sandwich and chewed in silence. The sound of chatter rose around them, and Latifah noticed other girls giggling and whispering. Perhaps, like the speaker had said that day, if the girls knew what Latifah and Maryam were doing right then, then Latifah and Maryam would be ashamed and inspired to repent.

"But how did she meet him in the first place?"

Maryam put a forkful of rice in her mouth and chewed before replying, her gaze avoiding Latifah's again. "He comes to the Muslim site to ask questions sometimes."

Right then, Latifah couldn't shake the feeling of deep disappointment in Maryam. She had expected more of her.

But, then again, hadn't she expected the same of herself?

***

"Friends forever, friends forever, friends forever more." Eyes shut and a grin lingering on her face, Maryam sat with her legs crossed under her as she held Samira's hands, their knees touching as they sat on Samira's bedroom floor.

It was a Friday evening in mid-March, and Basma was in the living room chatting with Joanne. It was rare that Basma visited Joanne, and Maryam suspected the visit was inspired by her mother's guilt in always asking Joanne and Samira to visit them.

"You first," Samira said after they opened their eyes. Samira's eyes twinkled in a way that made Maryam giggle in anticipation at what Samira would share during the heart-to-heart.

"Me?" Maryam laughed. "You always say that."

"Then go," Samira said, grinning. "And hurry up because I have something to share too."

Maryam rolled her eyes. "You always do."

Samira looked at Maryam, and it was obvious that her eagerness to hear Maryam's heart-to-heart was so they could move on to hers.

"Okay," Maryam said. "I wish I could go to public school."

Samira's eyebrows rose despite her restlessness to share her own secret. "Why?"

Maryam bit her lower lip before responding. "It's more fun than Muslim school."

"You see how Latifah's parents put her back in Muslim school? It's not as fun as you think."

"But you seem to like it."

"I hate it." Samira grimaced. "I wish we could afford Muslim school."

Maryam opened her mouth in surprise. "You do?"

"Of course. I hate looking like a weirdo, walking around in hijab." Samira sighed. "It was easier when Latifah was there."

"You didn't meet any other Muslims?"

"Two." Samira sucked her teeth. "But they don't count. One's a teacher. A man. And the other one doesn't cover, and she acts like I don't exist."

"That sucks."

"Sure does."

"But still…" Maryam said, eyes sad. "If I was there, we could wear hijab together."

Samira smacked Maryam's lap playfully then grasped Maryam's hands again as she closed her eyes. "My turn."

"Why are you shutting your eyes?" Maryam said. "We already did Friendship Style."

"Let's do it again."

"But why?"

"*Maryam.*" Samira opened her eyes as she stared at Maryam, annoyed. "Come on. Stop wasting time."

Samira shut her eyes again, and shrugging, Maryam followed suit.

"Friends forever, friends forever, friends forever more," they recited in unison.

"I'm going to meet him."

Maryam's eyes were still closed as Samira spoke. When she opened them, she met Samira's giddy expression with her eyebrows gathered.

"What?"

"Listen, Dummy." Samira tugged on Maryam's hand and smiled broadly, unable to keep from bouncing up and down in excitement at her news. "I'm going to meet him."

"Wh…when?" Maryam finally managed to say once she found her voice.

"Tomorrow."

"But… how?"

"At the mall, Dummy."

Maryam's eyes grew large. "You mean tomorrow, as in Saturday afternoon, when our parents drop us off?"

"Exactly."

Maryam's heart sank. She had planned this mall trip for weeks, having pleaded with her parents for the opportunity to go somewhere. They had agreed only because it was Spring Break and she wouldn't have any schoolwork due on Monday.

Maryam had asked Latifah to come along, but Latifah said her parents had some family barbeque they had to attend and Latifah was going with them. Of course, Maryam had invited Samira too, but she had never imagined that when Samira agreed, she had other plans in mind.

"...So you're just going to act normal, and I'll meet you in front of Nordstrom before they pick us up."

"What am I supposed to do while you—" Maryam looked at Samira, a thought coming to her suddenly. "Wait. Who are you meeting?"

Samira's shoulders slouched as her mouth fell open, her eyes reflecting hurt. "Are you even listening to me? I just told you that."

Maryam shook her head. "Sorry. I just..."

"Jason, Dummy. You know the cute guy whose website I showed you?"

"The one you're teaching about *Islam*?" Maryam hoped her sarcastic emphasis on the last word didn't escape her friend. Samira was out of her mind.

Samira waved her hand. "Yeah, whatever."

"I thought he lived in Florida."

"He's *from* Florida," Samira said, annoyance in her voice. "Gosh, Maryam. Do you listen to anything I say?"

"But the mall, Samira? That's crazy."

Samira contorted her face in offense. "And what's wrong with the mall? It's not like we'll be alone."

"Do you even hear yourself? This is totally *haraam*."

"Oh, you mean like replying to a private I-M?"

Maryam's cheeks colored. "Instant messaging isn't *haraam*. Anyway, I was—"

"Asking a question," Samira finished for, her tone flat.

Samira rolled her eyes. "Muslims like you are such hypocrites."

"*Samira*." Maryam's eyes reflected hurt more than offense.

"I'm serious. Everything's *haraam* except what *you* do."

"That's not true."

"It is. Look at you. You chat with boys online and pretend it's for Islam and then—"

"It *is* for Islam."

"—you tell me Facebook is *haraam* and I didn't even add boys."

"But you put pictures on Facebook."

"So? I didn't show them to boys."

"*I* never showed pictures to boys," Maryam said, exasperated.

"I didn't say you did. I'm just saying you make up rules to fit your life but—"

"I do *not*."

"—you say everything *I* do is wrong."

"That's not true."

"Then name one thing I do that you think is right."

An awkward silence followed as Samira crossed her arms, her eyes glistening in hurt as she regarded Maryam.

"I... I..." Maryam groped for an intelligent response, but she couldn't gather her thoughts. "I mean..."

Samira snorted. "Oh my God. You can't think of *one* thing good about me? Not even one thing?"

"Of course I can," Maryam said hurriedly. "I just..."

"You just what?"

"I...just never thought about it before, that's all."

Samira stared at Maryam for several seconds, but Maryam was at a loss for words. Samira's jaw quivered and her eyes shined with tears despite efforts to appear defiant and unperturbed.

"At least Jason cares about me." Samira's voice was shaky as she struggled to keep her composure. "Even if he's the only person in the world who does."

11

The Meeting

Saturday afternoon Maryam sat alone reading a book at a small table in the noisy food court of the mall. A half-eaten pretzel and a cup of cola were on a tray next to her though she had lost her appetite minutes after she bought the meal. She tried to concentrate on the words on the page in front of her, but her mind kept drifting to Samira.

"How do I look?" Samira had asked Maryam thirty minutes before as they stood in front of the bathroom mirrors in the mall.

Maryam had glanced at her friend and forced a smile, but her thoughts were distant and confused. "Great."

Samira rubbed the stick of gloss across her lips for the third time, leaning toward her reflection and smacking her lips. "Mww," she said jokingly, nudging Maryam in an apparent effort to get her to laugh.

Maryam had laughed despite herself, but she really felt like crying.

"Hmm..." Samira had said, turning left and right, looking doubtfully at her reflection. "This scarf makes me look like a dork."

"You look fine," Maryam had said, unable to muster the energy to make her tone match her words.

"Here."

The white cloth was balled up in Samira's hand before Maryam realized Samira had removed her hijab.

Maryam's eyes grew wide in protest, but the sound of a toilet flushing reminded her that they were not alone.

"What are you doing?" Maryam said in a harsh whisper.

"Here." Samira's eyes blinked impatiently, and Maryam groaned as she took the cloth from her friend's hands.

"And what am I supposed to do with this?" Maryam kept her voice low as a woman emerged from a stall.

"Put it in your purse, Dummy."

Maryam clinched her jaw as she opened her purse and stuffed the cloth inside. "I hate you."

Samira looked at her watch. "Oh my God. I'm late."

She took one last look in the mirror, ran her fingers through her hair and teased it to life before walking quickly toward the door that led back to the mall.

"Nordstrom. Five o'clock," she said, looking back before she rounded the corner and disappeared.

Presently, Maryam glanced at her watch. It was almost two thirty. She sighed, her head pounding in anxiety. What had she been thinking when she'd asked her parents to spend "all afternoon" at the mall? Of course, at the time, she had no idea she'd be spending it alone.

Maryam's stomach churned as she was reminded that even if she wanted to go shopping, each time she'd open her purse to pay for something, she'd see a white bundle stuffed in a corner of her handbag.

***

Maryam was only half-there at the mall that afternoon. She meandered through the corridors, stopping at every other store just to pass time.

"Oh my God. You can't think of one thing good about me? Not even one thing?"

What kind of horrible person are you? Maryam mentally scolded herself as she stood in front of a sales rack of colorful T-shirts and jean shorts, stuff she'd never wear. *Couldn't you have thought of one thing?*

But even then, as Maryam lifted a sleeveless shirt the color of vomit with red polka-dots allover and held it against the cloth of her *jilbaab* as she glanced down at herself, she couldn't think of a single good thing about Samira.

Idiot. That was the only word that described her friend.

Maryam's face grew hot in fury as she thought of how Samira had gotten her into this stupid mess. *O Allah. What if my parents find out? I'd be in so much trouble.* Why had she agreed to this dumb plan anyway? Her father was right. Americans were so irresponsible and stupid.

Muslims like you are such hypocrites.

What? Maryam tossed the polka-dot shirt on the rack, not bothering to put it back in its proper place. How dare Samira say something like that. How dare her. *She* was the hypocrite. Talking online with boys was not the same as meeting up with one!

But how did she meet him in the first place?

Maryam snorted as she recalled Latifah's judgmental tone at the lunch table that day. I bet she meets up with boys too, Maryam thought angrily.

"A boy asked for my phone number."

And Maryam recalled that Latifah didn't appear a bit ashamed when she'd said it. Latifah had actually been smiling.

Hypocrite. That's probably why her parents took her out of public school.

Don't you think you should tell her mom?

Oh, so now Latifah's the angel. Maryam readjusted her purse strap on her shoulder as she left the store, her heart a storm in her chest. No one had the right to judge her. She was a better Muslim than both of them. She didn't watch stupid movies like *Shrek* and *Incredibles*. She didn't have Facebook. She didn't take pictures of herself. She didn't wear hijabs with flower prints on them like they—

The shrill of a phone made Maryam start. She halted her steps as she looked around the mall's corridor in search of whose phone was ringing. The phone shrilled again just as she met the gaze of a guy who was staring at her, his face contorted. Her hand went to the cloth of her *khimaar* as she averted her gaze, feeling so small right then. She probably looked like a moron to him.

When the phone rang again, Maryam's heart raced, and she quickly opened her purse, remembering the phone her parents had given to her before dropping off her and Samira. It was an extra phone they kept for emergencies or whenever Maryam would be somewhere without them.

A sick feeling came over Maryam as she withdrew the white bundle to uncover the buried phone.

"Where are you?" Her mother's voice said before Maryam had the cell phone properly to her ear.

Maryam's heartbeat quickened as she stuffed the white cloth back into her purse, glancing about her nervously.

"Um…I'm here."

"Maryam." Her mother's tone was impatient. "I know you're here. But where? I told you to meet me in front of Nordstrom at five fifteen."

Maryam glanced at her wristwatch. It was 5:23. "Oh yeah. I'm on my way."

"On your way? I told you to be on time. We have a dinner at your uncle's house, and we have to drop off Samira before we get ready."

At the mention of Samira, Maryam's head throbbed. Samira was probably standing at Nordstrom now, fuming.

Oh my God. And what if Maryam's mother bumped into her? Maryam had Samira's *khimaar* in her purse!

"Okay. Coming." Maryam hung up and sped down the corridor, her palms growing sweaty as she grasped the phone. She speed-walked, running intermittently, as she made her way through the mall. Maryam hoped and prayed she would see Samira before her mother did.

When the sign for Nordstrom came into view, Maryam slowed her steps, her eyes wide in desperation as she scanned the spacious hall for her friend.

Come on, Samira. Come on, Samira. Come on!

When she didn't see Samira, Maryam's legs grew weak. Tears burned the back of her lids as she loitered outside the entrance, her heart thumping so violently that she felt it in her throat.

O Allah! Maryam's heart cried. *Please don't let my mom find her before I do.*

Maryam winced as the phone shrilled and vibrated in her palm. She stared at it, hesitating before answering it. Her mother's name was on the caller ID display, and Maryam knew her mother was getting hopelessly impatient. The phone rang again, but Maryam's arm was as if paralyzed.

"Allah forgive me," Maryam whispered, shutting her eyes. She pressed the button to refuse the call then held down the power button until the screen went black. Tears stung the back of her lids as she tucked the dead phone into her purse.

O Allah! Get me out of this, pleeeeeeease.

"Maryam!"

Maryam jerked her body around at the sound of her name. She was utterly petrified at the thought of looking her mother in the eye right then. Had she seen her turn off the phone?

"Maryam, don't touch that."

It took a second for Maryam to register a woman in hijab kneeling down and grabbing the pudgy hand of a three-year-old that was reaching for a display in the corridor near where Maryam stood.

"It's not a toy," the woman said, her voice fading as she stood and pushed the stroller along.

Maryam breathed a sigh of relief. But a second later, anxiety tightened in her chest as she realized she had no choice but to go inside Nordstrom, where she was sure Samira was waiting for her somewhere.

Maryam dragged her feet, the smell of perfume teasing her nostrils as she crossed the threshold of the store. Maryam saw her mother just as she passed the make-up display. Her mother stood to the side of the small corridor that led to the glass exit doors. Basma's contorted expression was apparent even though only her eyes were visible as she was looking at her cell phone and pressing a button with a gloved hand. Basma grunted in apparent frustration and before Maryam could duck behind a clothes rack, their eyes met.

Basma's eyes registered relief then scorn as she made her way toward Maryam. Maryam's shoulders' slouched as she realized that she wasn't going to get out of this after all. Her legs felt like lead as she slowly approached her mother.

"Where's Samira?" Basma snapped when Maryam stood in front of her.

Maryam averted her gaze, and tears welled in her eyes.

"What?" Basma's voice was on the verge of panic.

"I...I don't know." Maryam felt the weight of dread grow heavier in her chest, and the fear she'd suppressed the entire afternoon choked her as it became a tangible possibility.

"*What?*"

Maryam couldn't meet her mother's eyes that demanded a response. Her vision blurred and tears rounded her cheeks and dripped from her chin. But Maryam was too mentally exhausted to think of any logical response other than the truth.

12

Missing

"Top story tonight," the local news anchor said from the flashing screen of the Bilal family television set Monday night. The woman's face maintained an expression of obligatory concern as she looked into the camera. In a box next to the anchor's head was a smiling picture of Samira without hijab.

Latifah covered her face with her hands, and Rafiqah placed an arm around Latifah and drew her closer on the couch.

"Police are asking for any information about the whereabouts of a fifteen-year-old girl who was last seen just after two-o'clock on Saturday afternoon…"

***

"I told you this stupid charity of yours would end up hurting our family." Faris huffed as he stood leaning forward and gripping the back of the loveseat in the living room. He shook his head. "You and your crazy ideas."

Basma sat quietly on the couch with her reddened eyes cast down. Her shoulders were slumped, and her hands were folded loosely on her lap.

"I tell you, all these Americans bring is trouble. That could've been Maryam's face all over the news."

Basma heard her husband's voice as if coming from a distance, she was so consumed in her own anxiety and despair. The only voice she could hear clearly right then came from Joanne, who wouldn't leave her thoughts.

"How could you have let this happen?" Joanne had said late Saturday night at the mall. Then came Joanne's pitiful moan that dug into the flesh of Basma's chest and ripped her heart out. "Oh, I was so stupid to trust you." Basma's teeth had chattered in agony and helplessness as her limbs grew weak.

"O Allah! Bring her back." Joanne fell to her knees in the darkened corridor as the mall security stood by, apologetic expressions on their faces.

That was the last memory Basma had before everything went black.

Basma had woken on a couch, uncomfortable coldness stinging her head. When the room came into focus, she realized she was back at home, and her husband sat on an arm of the couch, holding an icepack against a side of her head.

***

"I know this a very difficult time for you, ma'am," the female police officer said for the third time. Her voice was steady as she sat a distance from Joanne on the couch. But Joanne sensed that the woman's patience was waning, evidenced by the male officer's shifting stance from where he stood near the front door, feet from the women. "But these questions are routine, and they will help clarify what most likely occurred."

Joanne exhaled as she tried to steady her asthmatic breaths. This all was still surreal to her. She was hoping the officers had come to tell her they had found Samira alive and well. But instead they started probing her about her private life and suggesting that Samira may have run away from home.

But Samira would never do that. Never. Joanne needed her too much.

***

"Police are not responding to questions about who owns the website of the man the missing teen allegedly said she was going to meet Saturday afternoon. But sources say that it is not registered under the name of anyone by the name of 'Jason' and that the pictures of the young man on the site are not those of the site owner, who sources say is more than fifty years old."

***

"Latest developments in the case of the missing teen: Local police have taken into custody two men, one eighteen, the other fifty-two, believed to be connected to the disappearance of the teen who has been missing now for six days. Right now, police are not giving any further information and are not saying whether or not the men are being charged with a crime."

***

"Breaking news. Sources say police have discovered the whereabouts of a teen who witnesses say fits the description of the fifteen-year-old who has been missing now for eight days. Police are not saying whether or not the girl is Samira Saadiq or how or where she was found, or if she's in good condition."

13

Questions Answered

"All I ask of you, Joanne, is that you don't blame Samira for what happened." Gregory, Joanne's younger brother, stood with his hands in the pockets of his jeans near the front door of Joanne's home. "She's been through enough this week."

It was Monday afternoon, nine days after Samira had disappeared, and Samira now sat slouched on the couch of the living room of her home, her eyes cast down. She had arrived home an hour before with her uncle, who had voluntarily brought Samira into the police station when he realized that she had been reported missing.

"I..." Joanne's breath caught as her mind struggled to grasp that her daughter was alive and well. "Thank you, Greg." It was all she could do to keep from breaking down.

He nodded, but Joanne could tell her brother's mind was on assuring her that Samira was fine. "I had no idea she was even at my house," Gregory said. "Amy and I had traveled for the weekend, and apparently Carrie let her stay in her room the whole time."

Carrie was Gregory and Amy's sixteen-year-old daughter who had kept in touch with Samira over the years. Joanne remembered seeing Carrie listed as one of Samira's Facebook friends when Joanne discovered the account in Saudi Arabia.

"I'm sure you already know that she's unharmed," he said. "The young man named Jason had no idea any of this occurred. But apparently, he was the one who dropped Samira off at my house after she left the mall."

Joanne drew in a deep breath and exhaled. Pain knotted in her head from all the stress. Yes, the police had told her the same version of events. The website that was rumored to be owned by someone other than Jason was Jason's after all; it had simply been registered and purchased by his father on his behalf, inciting rumors that Samira had been abducted by a fifty-year-old man.

"What I don't know," Gregory said as he looked at his niece, sadness in his eyes, "is why she felt she couldn't come home last Saturday."

Samira glanced at her mother tentatively, her eyes registering nervousness, as if afraid her mother would ask her to explain right then. But Joanne turned to her brother.

"Thank you, Greg. I can't tell you how happy I am that she was with you the whole time."

"I am too, Joanne. And it's a blessing that Jason is an honest kid." Gregory was looking at Samira then, and Joanne sensed he meant for Samira to hear his every word.

"I hope Samira knows many people on the other side of the internet are predators of young girls," he said. "She just got lucky. I hope she doesn't do anything like this again. People don't often get lucky twice." He pursed his lips. "Most people don't even get lucky once."

***

"While I was waiting for Maryam, I saw Sister Basma come in," Samira said from where she sat at the kitchen table across from her mother late that night. Her gaze was averted as she spoke, and her voice was low, as if nervous about speaking about what had happened. But Joanne was relieved that Samira was talking at all.

"Maryam was supposed to meet me at five o'clock, but she was late. I was scared Sister Basma would see me without hijab, so I ran."

"But why didn't you just come home, sweetheart?"

"I was going to, but..." Samira looked up at her mother, ashamed. "...I was scared you'd be home, and Maryam had my *khimaar*."

"But why a whole week?" Joanne shook her head, confounded. "That's a long time."

Samira cast her eyes down. "Carrie said maybe it was better if I stayed with them for awhile."

Joanne squinted her eyes in confusion. "All of this because you were scared you'd get in trouble?"

Samira nodded hesitantly, her eyes welling with tears. "I didn't want you to look at me like Maryam's family did. I wanted you to think I was good."

"And you thought that making one mistake would make you bad?"

Samira shook her head as tears slipped down her cheeks. She wiped them away with the palms of her hands. "I thought you'd think I was never good in the first place."

Joanne shut her eyes slowly as tears filled her own eyes.

"And if...if..." Samira sniffed, her voice cracking. "And if Dad found out..." She whimpered. "...he might never come back to us again."

14

Homecoming

It was a Saturday night in early July and the prayer hall of the masjid was filled with friends, family, and acquaintances of Joanne and Riaz Saadiq. In the woman's prayer area, Samira beamed as she sat next to Latifah on the carpeted floor. She squeezed Latifah's hand in excitement.

"Tell your mom congratulations," Latifah said, smiling back at her friend. "I'm happy for you. I just wish they weren't taking you back to Saudi Arabia."

Samira bounced up and down in excitement as she sat with her legs folded under her, barely hearing Latifah right then. "My parents are getting married."

Latifah laughed. "Yeah, I know. We got the invitation a month ago."

Rafiqah had told Latifah that Samira's father had panicked when he heard of Samira's disappearance. He had tried desperately to get a flight to the States, but none were available that would allow him to arrive before three weeks time. He reserved the earliest flight he could then spent what time he could at the *Ka'bah* in Makkah, crying and begging Allah for Samira's safe return—and his own forgiveness. Apparently, he blamed himself for Samira's disappearance, believing that Allah was punishing him for breaking up his family for no valid reason. So he swore to Allah that if Samira returned home unharmed, he'd remarry Joanne and bring his wife and daughter back with him to Saudi Arabia.

"This is soooo cool," Samira said, bouncing up and down again as her eyes sparkled.

"I know." Latifah nodded. "It is, isn't it?"

A smile lingered on Latifah's face. "When is your flight?"

"Monday night."

Latifah's expression grew sad. She would miss Samira. After the abduction scare, Latifah and Samira had grown closer, especially after Maryam's father forbade Maryam from seeing Samira again. Though Latifah was still allowed to visit Maryam, Latifah's family was rarely invited over anymore, but Latifah wasn't bothered too much. She and Maryam spent a lot of time together at school—at least before the school year ended a couple of weeks ago.

"If Brother Faris wasn't friends with your father," Rafiqah had said to Latifah the day Joanne told her that Faris was forbidding his daughter from seeing Samira, "I think we'd be forbidden too."

"But why?" Latifah's eyes were full of hurt and confusion.

"Everybody has their struggles, sweetheart. Lord knows I have mine." She frowned thoughtfully. "But I think Brother Faris's biggest fear is that his daughter will become Americanized."

"But..."

"I know it doesn't make sense to us." Rafiqah shook her head. "But to be fair, I think I understand where he's coming from."

Latifah creased her forehead in confusion, taken aback by her mother's words. "You do?"

"I don't agree with his decision, of course," Rafiqah said. "But America is a strange country to him, so he's doing what he can to protect his family."

"But he's lived here a long time."

"But his heart and mind are still in Pakistan."

Latifah wrinkled her nose. "That's not good."

Rafiqah's eyes registered disagreement. "We can't say that. I imagine if we moved to Saudi Arabia like Joanne's family, our hearts and minds would still be in America. And that's not necessarily bad."

Latifah's expression reflected bewilderment, as she was unable to grasp how her mother could defend what Brother Faris had done.

"Sweetheart, when Allah allows us to love across cultures, it forces us to see the world through different eyes."

A hesitant grin creased a corner of Latifah's mouth. "You love Sister Basma's family?"

"Absolutely. Very much."

"Even after what they did to Samira?"

Rafiqah drew in a deep breath and exhaled, a shadow of a smile lingering on her face. "Yes, I do."

Latifah drew her eyebrows together more. "But…"

"We're all human, sweetheart. If you start thinking someone isn't worthy of being loved because of their mistakes, then you've missed the entire message of Islam."

"How?"

"Remember the hadith from Bukhari that your father hung on the wall of our living room?"

Latifah's forehead was creased as she thought for a moment. Seconds later, her expression relaxed as she recalled the framed print-out that she barely paid attention to.

If anyone testifies that none has the right to be worshipped except Allah Alone Who has no partners, and that Muhammad is His Slave and His Messenger, and that Jesus is Allah's Slave and His Messenger and His Word which He bestowed on Mary and a Spirit created by Him, and that Paradise is true, and Hell is true, Allah will

admit him into Paradise with the deeds which he had
done, even if those deeds were few.

Latifah had lowered her head as she thought of her own dying hope of entering Paradise when she died. For months she had carried with her the deadweight of guilt until it numbed her. She recalled the warm feeling that had tickled her when Kendrick picked her up and squeezed her hand. Whenever the Islamic studies teacher at the Muslim school talked about striving for Paradise, Latifah felt a lump in her throat, regret paralyzing her.

Paradise wasn't for people like her, Latifah would think sadly, her elbow propped on her desk and her fist against her cheek as she doodled in the corner of her Islamic studies notebook.

The teacher would recite *ayaat* from the Qur'an about Allah's mercy and forgiveness, and Latifah would feel something stirring inside her, but she feared that her good deeds were too few to allow her to be admitted to Paradise.

Allah will admit him into Paradise with the deeds which he had done, even if those deeds were few.

Tears gathered in Latifah's eyes as the deadweight of sin lightened in her chest. *SubhaanAllah.* There was hope for her after all.

And for all Muslims.

EPILOGUE

Maryam's Thoughts

Have you ever wanted something so badly you could scream? That's how I felt when my parents threw away the wedding invitation and said I couldn't speak to Samira anymore.

Latifah said everybody was in tears at the masjid that day. She said even Mr. Butt and his family came!

I cried when I imagined Samira all giddy because her parents were getting back together. When I closed my eyes, I could see Samira's sparkling eyes as she bounced up and down because she couldn't sit still.

Latifah said Brother Riaz even got on the microphone and thanked everybody for praying for them when they couldn't find Samira.

Uff! I think my parents are being totally unreasonable blaming Samira for everything. We were both wrong. I know that now.

...And it makes me wonder who I really am deep inside.

Maybe I'll never know.

But one thing's for sure, I'm going to try hard to stay away from trouble. And I'll start by obeying my parents from now on, inshaaAllah, and praying salaat as soon as it comes in...like Samira always did.

But I don't know what I'll do without Samira around. I swear, she won't leave my heart, no matter what I do. I can still hear her saying, "Friends forever, friends forever, friends forever more..."

Latifah says don't stress too much though. She says if I'm patient, inshaaAllah, we'll all be together in Jannah.

I laughed when she said that. I mean, I know it sounds weird, but I'd never thought of Paradise as something to really look forward to.

But I do now.

If we go to Paradise, I think I'll tell Samira to stop asking us to chant that silly Friendship Style. I don't think we'll need any silly promises like that to make sure we stay friends.

Because, in Paradise, Allah will make our hearts love each other anyway, and it won't matter what we think.

ALSO BY UMM ZAKIYYAH

If I Should Speak

A Voice

Footsteps

Realities of Submission

Hearts We Lost

Muslim Girl

UZ Short Story Collection

His Other Wife

ABOUT THE AUTHOR

Daughter of American converts to Islam, Umm Zakiyyah, also known by her birth name Ruby Moore, is the award-winning author of the *If I Should Speak* trilogy and *Muslim Girl.*

Umm Zakiyyah's books have been used in schools and universities in America and abroad for multicultural and religious studies. She writes about the interfaith struggles of Muslims and Christians, and the intercultural, spiritual, and moral struggles of Muslims in America.

She currently resides in Washington, D.C.

Visit **ummzakiyyah.com** or **uzauthor.com** to find out more about the author.